RECHARGE

RECHARGE

NEW EDEN BOOK 3

JESSICA MARTING

SHADOW PRESS

Recharge (New Eden Book 3)

ISBN 978-1-989780-38-1

Edited by Autumn Reed

Cover design by German Creative

Content notes: Discussion of a natural disaster and mass casualty event; discussion of and flashbacks of intimate partner violence and animal cruelty.

For David

RODELLE KEPT her eyes on the kitchen counter, its smooth wood scarred from decades of use and reuse. Behind her, Jackson threw an empty glass bottle against the wall. It landed centimeters from her head, where it shattered, spraying its remaining drops of dandelion wine across the cracked tile floor. Tomorrow, he would be angry that the bottle was broken, with glassware in short supply on New Eden. Her entire body tensed as she tried not to flinch, hoping he would direct his anger elsewhere, even though she knew hoping was futile.

"I'm sick of this," Jackson seethed.

Rodelle closed her eyes, waiting for his hand to grip her shoulder, to whirl her around and strike her face. She held her breath, the skin between her shoulder blades itching in horrible anticipation . . .

Her eyes fluttered open. Heart in her throat, she gazed at the ceiling, her vision slow to focus. It took a few seconds for her to catch her breath as she realized where she was—the dilapidated shed in her backyard that her late husband had pretentiously referred to as "the guesthouse." She'd had that dream again. Terror still gripped her, as fiercely as Jackson's hand used to around her wrists and neck.

Outside her open window, she heard Brandon singing softly to himself, off-key as usual. Sunlight streamed through the threadbare curtains as they bobbed gently in the breeze, a reminder that she had made a new start. The entire planet had, thanks to Brandon and the rest of his cyborg friends. New Eden finally had a chance at rebuilding itself. Brandon and some of his fellow cyborgs had just returned from their first-ever off-world supply run the day before, bringing necessities and luxuries that Rodelle had never expected to see in her lifetime.

She pushed aside her thin sheet and crawled out of her makeshift bed, a mattress stuffed with rags and old straw on the bare floor. An earthenware cup of water waited on the floor next to it, and she gulped it down. She reminded herself that she had a lot to look forward to now, not just a future without Jackson.

"Hey, are you awake?" Brandon's voice sounded almost irritating in its cheerfulness, and if he'd been anyone else, Rodelle would have been annoyed at his being a morning person. As it was, his cybernetically enhanced hearing would have detected her getting up. Maybe her changing breathing patterns too. She wondered if he had been able to hear that she'd been having a nightmare. She hoped not.

"Yeah." Her voice sounded creaky from sleep, and she cleared her throat. She crossed the small space to the structure's open window to see Brandon standing over the firepit in her backyard, a pot hanging over it on a cobbled-together tripod. He wore nothing but the regulation black flight trousers the other cyborgs wore, revealing his toned back and chest for all to see. Or at least Rodelle, whose breath caught for half a second, as it always did when she saw him shirtless. God above, he was an attractive man.

She quickly regained her composure. "What are you up to? The electricity's working in my kitchen. We don't have to cook over fires anymore."

"What I'm making tastes best when cooked over an open fire. We brought back some meat stores. Want a piece of naroki for breakfast?" He held out a hand with a flourish, as if they were in a high-tech gourmet kitchen on a deep space waystation instead of her ramshackle backyard. Although, come to think of it, a waystation probably wouldn't have a kitchen at all, but fancy food replicators.

"I don't know what naroki is."

"They roam the planets in the Eckler Cluster on six legs, biting and hissing at anyone who looks at them sideways. One of the most edible bastards you'll ever taste. Well, technically, this is a cloned bastard, but it all tastes the same when it's been slow-roasted over a fire." Brandon tilted his head to the side, waiting for her answer.

Her heart skipped a beat at the gesture and the open expression on his face, like he hoped she would like whatever he had prepared. She smiled. "That sounds lovely, actually."

"I have coffee and tea cubes too. I managed to snag a few from the ship's cargo bay before anyone noticed. They're on the kitchen counter. All you have to do is pour boiling water over them."

She blinked in surprise. "Real coffee?"

"Technically, it's synthesized. I don't know of anywhere in this part of the galaxy that has old-world coffee plants." He looked apologetic.

Rodelle wouldn't know the difference, never having tasted coffee before. "That doesn't matter to me. Do you want some?"

"If you're already boiling water, a cup of tea would be great, thanks."

She nodded and stepped away, draping the curtain over the window. On bare feet, she padded across the yard, past Brandon, and through the open door to the kitchen. She filled her dented kettle from the water pump in the sink, then placed it on a hot plate, powered by one of the cyborgs' weird everlasting batteries.

While the water boiled, she picked up an unfamiliar package resting on the counter. Unsealing it with her fingernail, she opened it to see an array of paper-wrapped cubes, labeled with different names of coffee and tea. The scents were heavenly, curious mixes of sweet, spices, and moss. They definitely smelled more appealing than the dandelion tea New Eden had been drinking since before Rodelle was born. Brandon hadn't specified which tea he wanted, so she picked one that smelled of wood and citrus, then dropped the cube in a metal cup with a curved handle. She put a random coffee cube in a matching cup, then took care to fold the packaging, the habit to save everything that could be reused still deeply ingrained in her.

She poured boiling water over them as Brandon instructed. The smells were incredible, unlike anything she'd ever come across before. Anticipation welled up in her, both at trying something new and having a leisurely breakfast with Brandon. Meals with him had been an unexpected and very welcome perk since his ship landed in an untended field in the middle of the night, months ago.

She'd even stopped feeling guilty about spending more time with him than Hannah and Jasmine, her lifelong friends. Both of them were occupied with their cyborg boyfriends, anyway—two of them, in Jasmine's case. Rodelle was pleased that their relationships seemed to be going much better than the disastrous one she'd shared with Jackson.

Thinking of Jackson made her think of her nightmare, and her happiness flagged a little. Standing in the doorway that led to the backyard, she reminded herself that Jackson was long dead. Crushed under bricks in the old community center when it collapsed in the last major earthquake, his body buried in a cemetery a kilometer away. Dead and gone, forever.

Death shouldn't cheer her, not after she'd seen so much of it in her thirty-four years living in New Eden. Especially not when the dead person in question had been her husband. But it did. Rodelle wouldn't be making the mistake that was marriage ever again.

"Everything okay?"

Brandon's voice snapped her out of her reverie, and she nearly dropped the cups. "Fine, thank you." She forced herself to smile, to remember where she was, who she was with—her charming cyborg boarder, who lived in the main house she had once shared with Jackson. She'd been happy to turn it over to Brandon when he and his cyborg brethren needed places to stay.

She handed the tea to him. "I didn't know which one you liked," she said. She took a cautious sip of her coffee, flinching at its heat. Best to wait a few minutes.

He shrugged. "I'm not fussy. Thank you." He bestowed a smile on her. Those smiles always managed to do something to her, making her stomach flutter in a way no one else's had.

She knew what it was—she was lusting after him, after someone for possibly the first time in her life. It was an emotion she kept carefully tucked away, not even discussing her crush with Jasmine and Hannah. She had only recently been able to acknowledge it to herself. "You're welcome. How's the naroki coming along?"

"Just about done." He flashed a grin at her. "I hope you're hungry."

Her stomach reminded her that she was. She hoped he didn't hear it growling. Sitting down in one of the wooden chairs in front of the firepit, she watched Brandon carefully maneuver chunks of brown meat marbled with golden stripes on a pair of hammered metal plates. He placed one in front of her on the tiny table between the chairs. "You came prepared," she said.

"I can't be a good host without tableware, can I?"

"I thought I was the host. Hostess," she corrected herself.

"I'm cooking one of my favorite meals for you, so that makes me the host." He sat down across from her. "Try it."

She did, then tried not to moan as the taste and texture hit her. It was a blend of smoke and seasonings her palate didn't recognize, with a hint of sweetness underneath as the meat fell apart in her mouth. "Oh, my God," she murmured. "This is incredible." She ate another mouthful. So much better than anything she'd eaten in years. "You said the naroki are mean?"

"Rudest and stupidest animals in the galaxy. They eat and destroy everything."

"So, I don't have to feel guilty about eating them like I do with chickens."

"No. I get that. Chickens are kind of cute."

Rodelle immediately wished she hadn't brought up chickens. She thought about her pet hen, Gracie, which made her think about what Jackson had done to Gracie shortly after they married. Her heart still hurt when she thought of the bird. She swallowed some coffee, needing to change the subject. "Oh!" she said in surprise as its taste registered.

"Is that a good *oh* or a bad *oh*?"

That would be a good way to segue into a dirty joke if she had the courage to tell them. "A good one," she said. "It's bitter, but it's not? I'm not sure how to describe it." She drank some more.

"I'm glad you like it." He beamed at her from across the table. He shifted in his seat, the movement causing his knee to bump hers. Despite his wearing trousers, she felt the touch against her bare leg as acutely as if it had been skin-to-skin. Goose bumps pebbled along her arms. If he noticed, she hoped he thought it was because of the breeze. He leaned forward, an uncharacteristically serious expression on his face. "There's something I wanted to talk to you about."

She felt her stomach drop out, a stupid sensation. Was he moving out? It would pain her to see him leave, but if he wanted to . . . "What is it?" she asked, injecting as much affability into her voice as she could.

"Nothing too serious, I hope. At least, nothing that would affect us now. Rhys told us on our shared link that he thinks the original settlers probably weren't the technophobic zealots everyone thinks them to be. He said he found evidence in the comms tower. Didn't go into too many details. I guess they'll talk about it at the meeting this morning." He took a deep swallow of tea.

Shock suffused her body at that bit of information he'd so casually thrown out. "What kind of evidence? The comms tower has been a wreck for years!"

He shrugged. "I don't know yet. A meeting has been called at the amphitheater later this morning to talk about it."

Rodelle sighed. "Usually, I'd complain about yet another meeting, but I can't blame Rhys and everyone for wanting to hold one."

"Your people like meetings." He flashed a smile at her over the rim of his cup.

"I guess they're *our* people now, and yeah, they do."

"Better than a dictatorship and unilateral decision-making."

She nodded. Not for the time, she wondered how Jackson would have handled the cyborgs' arrival. He almost certainly wouldn't have cooperated with them the way the remaining New Edeners had. He would have done something stupid to show off in front of them or assert his authority, then ended up dying in a way more painful than how he actually had.

She closed her eyes, as if doing so would erase the memory of his death. She had never spoken about it before, and she wasn't about to start now.

"Rodelle? You're spacing out."

Brandon's voice had her opening her eyes again. "Sorry," she said, then took a bite of the naroki meat. "This is delicious. Thank you again. You'll have to show me how to roast this sometime."

"It's almost enough to make you wish you went along to the waystation, isn't it?"

"Sort of. Jasmine tagged along, and considering everything that happened onboard, I'm kind of glad I didn't."

He looked like he was fighting not to laugh. "Yeah, I can see how that would be weird. It was definitely a little awkward."

"I hope none of them were logged into your brain network thing at the time."

That remark earned a smile from Brandon, bright as the suns' rays. "No."

"I'm happy for them," Rodelle emphasized. "I really am. But I imagine things can get weird really quickly when you're in close quarters with three people who are . . . well, you know."

"Fucking their way through space?"

"Yes." She felt herself blush and hoped he didn't notice.

Brandon rose, cup in hand. "It can get weird. I'm going to take care of the cleanup, then head over to the amphitheater."

Surprised by the abrupt change in subject, Rodelle stood too. "Let me help."

"Don't worry about it, it's my mess. It'll only take a few minutes. Why don't you get dressed, and we'll head to the amphitheater together?"

"Sure." Rodelle drained the last of her coffee. "I won't be long."

As she returned to the house, she wondered where the conversation had gone sideways. Had she breached some kind of cyborg etiquette? Sighing, she placed her cup in the sink and headed to her guesthouse to get ready.

CHAPTER TWO

IT WAS good to see Rodelle's eyes lose their haunted look for a little while, to see her cracking jokes. She had come out of her shell in recent days, something Brandon was only too happy to see. He was certain her friends were pleased to see her relax a little too.

But his thoughts about her smile, her rare laugh, evaporated from his mind as he processed what Rhys was saying on the amphitheater stage: the original New Eden settlers may not have fled to this obscure backwater five stops past the edge of nowhere simply to escape modern amenities, like terraformed planets and hospitals. The destruction to the comms tower was too deliberate, as if someone expected that, eventually, it would have to be put back together without new components. It was likely why Hannah had been able to cobble together a workable system to send out an SOS all those months ago. Almost all the parts she'd needed had been already there, waiting for someone to piece them together like a jigsaw puzzle.

The meeting brought the news that there was another puzzle to solve: what could be waiting in the northern part of New Eden's single landmass. Rhys had the notion that its cave network could be hiding evidence of criminal activity of the original settlers. It sounded a little far-fetched to Brandon, but he wasn't in charge. He wasn't even cloned from a soldier or spy, like the other cyborgs. Brayden Emerson—his original—had been a cook or chef, something to do with hospitality. Brandon didn't care to think too closely about that man or his motivations for joining such a terrible cause.

Rhys ended the meeting by calling for volunteers to make an expedition to the north, warning that it would have to be on foot, due to the lack of ground transportation on New Eden. Three or four days each way, Brandon guessed. Hell of a trip on a place as low-tech as this one.

The crowd had started to disperse when Rodelle touched Brandon's hand. The motion sent a frisson of electricity through him, as it always did whenever they touched. His breath stilled for a second. "I think I want to go on the expedition," she said quietly.

He hadn't been expecting that. "Really? It's going to take a few days."

"I've never been anywhere but the settlement before. Jasmine got to ride in your spaceship. I want my own adventure." She sounded resolved, as though she'd already decided what she wanted to do and to hell with everyone who said it might not be a good idea.

"You don't have to justify wanting to go to me," Brandon said.

Both of them were quiet as they walked back to the Lansing house, though the silence was a comfortable one. Brandon thought about how empty her home would be with Rodelle away, despite spending the bulk of her time in the small house in the backyard. Its window was open to the elements, and it drove him crazy that she wouldn't stay in her house, even though he had offered to switch. She always demurred, insisting that New Eden's mild climate and lack of insects and predators meant she was fine to essentially sleep outside.

A very small insect population and almost no native fauna species. Those details had stuck out to Brandon from the moment they landed on the planet. According to Hannah Forsyth, New Eden once had bird and fish populations, but they'd been decimated years ago. Brandon wasn't sure how the original settlers would have the foresight to bring poultry from their home planet and take great care of them to make sure their population didn't die out while hunting the native species to extinction. Like other things about New Eden's history, it didn't make sense.

He didn't believe there would be answers or evidence in the north. Brandon had the sneaking suspicion that any of that would have been destroyed or forgotten about, that this mission would be a waste of time. But if Rodelle wanted to make the journey . . . "I think I'd like to go too," he announced, surprising himself.

She brightened. "You do?"

He nearly backtracked, but the hopeful look on her face bolstered him. "Why not? I've seen the same five square kilometers of this settlement dozens of times, and I'm bored of it. I can't imagine how you feel."

"Bored and restless, mostly. As much as I'd like to stick around and help build the hospital, I don't know what the hell I'm doing with the supplies you brought back from the waystation."

An earthquake-proof hospital would be constructed soon, a vast upgrade from the small clinic that had been destroyed in the quake. "It'll probably be done by the time we get back. We're using a pre-fab structure for it."

"Then all we need is a doctor." Before Brandon could point out that there was a medic in the cyborg ranks thanks to CW44, Rodelle added, "Maybe there's a doctor or two on the nearest waystation who will want to move." The ship was scheduled to make another supply run within the next couple of days.

Speaking of moving, Brandon couldn't help but ask, "Are you sure you want to go on the trip to the north? It's going to be a lot rougher than a visit to the waystation."

She shrugged. "It's not like a tiger will come out of nowhere and eat me."

"What's a tiger?"

"An extinct old-world giant cat. I've only seen pictures of them."

Brandon racked his memory files, trying to conjure an image of what a giant cat would look like. Come to think of it, he couldn't imagine what a small cat looked like, either. "I'm unfamiliar with the species altogether."

"So am I, aside from the stories I used to hear from my grandparents. The original settlers brought a few house cats with them, but there weren't any vermin for them to hunt, and I guess no one thought to recruit a veterinarian for the settlement, I don't know. Anyway, that's why we don't have pets."

There was a slight hitch to her voice when she spoke the last words, something Brandon wouldn't have picked up on without his enhanced senses. "Did I hit a sore spot with you?" he asked.

She barked out a harsh laugh that rang false. "No, not at all. Look, I noticed some interesting ingredients this morning when I was getting our coffee and tea. What did you manage to filch from the ship?"

Brandon *had* touched a nerve with his chatter about pets. Rodelle tended to change the subject when she was confronted with something she wasn't ready to talk about, and he always took her hints. "I did not filch. I asked for enough samples to test out a recipe or two that New Eden hasn't seen before. I have a bit of flour, some cooking oil, that kind of thing. All synthesized, of course. The real stuff is too expensive in this part of the galaxy. I was going to bake something to share."

She brightened, a spark appearing in her eyes that he loved to see. "Can I help?"

The thought of whiling away a couple of hours with her in a kitchen held a great deal of appeal. "Of course. Have you had doughnuts before?"

———

IT WAS a little unsettling to be back in the kitchen for longer than it took to grab a couple of tea cubes. It always was. Rodelle hoped that Brandon didn't notice her reaction as he set out the ingredients for doughnuts and she hunted for her great-grandmother's cookbook stash. He'd been surprised to learn that she knew what they were, although she'd never had the ingredients or inclination to bake them before. He chattered about baking times and appliances she had never heard of, let alone seen, as he set up the small convection oven that had been in her family since their arrival on New Eden. She leafed through one of the cookbooks and read some of the descriptions of the recipes aloud, amused at his incredulity at the foodstuffs. It was nice; the kitchen hadn't been a place of happy memories during her marriage.

"Some of the components are wearing out, but I've jerry rigged them with one of the solar batteries until they can be replaced," Brandon finally said when the oven was ready. The heat coils on the stovetop glowed red.

Rodelle blinked and pasted a smile to her face. "What was that? Sorry, I was woolgathering."

"Your oven is fine for now, but its days are numbered. You need a new one." Brandon looked around the kitchen thoughtfully. "Have you thought about renovating your kitchen entirely? You can do that now."

Hope and desire seized Rodelle at the notion of tearing out everything in her home that reminded her of Jackson. "I *could* do that."

"Are you very attached to the oven? It's pretty old."

She waved her hand, as if to dismiss the old thing herself. "Not at all. I'm afraid I'm not going to be of much help during this lesson. I haven't had a lot of opportunities to make anything extravagant."

He raised an eyebrow at her choice of words, a smile quirking his lips. Her heart skipped a beat at the sight, and she felt a blush creep up her neck and cheeks. "I suppose desserts fall under that category."

"Did you bake on your asteroid settlement?"

He shrugged, then measured out some flour in a bowl that hadn't come from Rodelle's cupboard. "There wasn't much of a chance to do that. We had replicators and synthesizers in our dome. I also have reason to believe that I'm one of the only people who cares about things like texture and seasoning, compared to the others."

"Did your original cook?" The question slipped out before she could stop herself. "Sorry, I know that's personal."

He shrugged, clearly unperturbed. "I think so, if my innate abilities out of the cloning tank are anything to go by." He added some yeast to the flour from a small plasti-glas bottle, then cracked a couple of eggs into the bowl. "Do you have any sugar berries for the topping?"

"Yeah, I made them into a jam, though. That should work, right?"

"Perfect. Saves us some time." He sent another heart-stopping grin her way. She had to remind herself to breathe, to look through the cupboard for the jar of jam she'd stored there, its glass permanently cloudy. "I don't think my original was a soldier," he continued. "I'm pretty sure Brayden Emerson was a chef, someone pretentious and short on money for him to sign up for a cyborg project. I don't have a lot of flashbacks or 'memory shards,' as Rhys likes to call them. When I do get them, they're usually of me standing in a hot kitchen, so I think my previous clones were cooks, too, once the others figured out I'm useless in battle."

His answer, so casual and unlike the guarded ones the other cyborgs tended to give, only brought up more questions for Rodelle. "Why do you think Brayden was pretentious? And give me that bowl. I can stir dough just fine."

"Blend. You're going to blend the dough," he corrected her before handing over the bowl. "I've always had an affinity for good ingredients. Wine too. I only work with synthesized food if I have to. I can't tell you how much I'm looking forward to preparing and eating real meat, having enough time to tenderize it the way it's supposed to be done. I've never seen a range in my life, but I remember knowing what one was a couple of weeks after I got out of the cloning tank." He looked around the kitchen. "Do you have any loose sugar berries? I want to see if I can dehydrate a few. I think their fat content will help make up for the lack of butter in this batch. If nothing else, New Eden should be proud of their planet's ability to produce fruit with fat content."

"I think I already have dehydrated berries in here somewhere." Rodelle wrenched open a drawer under the counter, one that always stuck, and took out a small jar of ground sugar berries. A greasy film clung to the inside of the jar, the result of the berries' fat composition. "What's a range?"

"A kind of stove mostly used in professional kitchens and those belonging to rich people. I think Brayden might have worked with one that used natural gas, maybe? I'm not sure."

The term meant nothing to Rodelle. "Oh." Food had only ever been a source of fuel for her for as long as she could remember. New Eden could grow crops that had been brought over from the old world: carrots, potatoes, corn, and tomatoes had been dietary staples since the settlement was established. According to Hannah, who had pored over old records when she started working in the agri-center, the soil didn't lend itself to much of the fruit species the original settlers imported.

Thinking of those records reminded Rodelle that they had been in the community center, now long gone in the quake. *Gone, along with Jackson.* She barely suppressed a shudder. The feeling was quickly replaced by a combination of relief and shame.

"Everything okay?" Brandon asked. "You kind of zoned out there for a sec."

She shook her head a little, clearing away the proverbial cobwebs. "I'm fine. Do we have to adjust the dough's rising time at all? I'm used to working with yeast substitutes."

"My condolences." Brandon peered into the bowl. "You'll have to tell me about what you used for substitutes sometime, though. I think this is fine to leave as is, but we'll keep an eye on it, anyway. I don't know how well the sugar berries are going to cooperate with the yeast, or how quickly the dough's going to rise with the humidity."

"You mean, you don't have high-tech cyborg yeast that makes things rise in seconds?"

Brandon paused, as if considering her words. "You know, that's not a bad idea. Once we've got the hospital and spaceport built, New Eden in better shape—genetically modified yeast isn't a bad project to start."

"It could be a whole new hobby for you, if you don't mind having to work with synthesized food."

"Who knows? In a few years, New Eden might be a brand new culinary capital of the galaxy. Besides, I don't count genetically modified yeast as synthesized."

Not too long ago, Rodelle would have despaired just thinking about what life on New Eden would be like—perpetual heat and humidity, broken up by a too-short rainy season, supplies rapidly dwindling, a tiny population ready to kill each other before starvation or natural disasters could. As fanciful as Brandon's words about such a remote place becoming known for its culinary fare were, his optimism buoyed Rodelle's spirits. The good things he and his cyborg brethren brought to New Eden had brought her back in a way she never expected.

"Maybe someday," Rodelle agreed. "I've never been to a restaurant before, though. You?"

"Not yet. Do you think your friends would want to try some of these? We have enough dough for a dozen doughnuts, and I don't think we can eat them all before they spoil. We'll need outside opinions too."

"Hannah and Jasmine would definitely eat these, yeah." She peered at the cookbook's faded type. "How do you want to fry them?"

"The stovetop will do, if we're careful. If the first one is a dud, we'll fry them over the firepit. I want to see what your oven can do for pastries." He looked at the bowl, as if expecting to see the dough to rise, then at the oven, nearly warmed up, thanks to the batteries. "Can I take a look at the rest of your recipes? You have quite the stash."

"I have more books in my . . ." She nearly said *bedroom*, but that space hadn't been hers in years. Brandon had taken to sleeping in the cramped living room since he'd moved in, waving off her offers of taking her room. "The bedroom," she finished.

She avoided it as much as possible. When she entered it this time, it didn't feel so oppressive as it had when she and Jackson still used it. The scents of dust and disuse clung to the air, but the atmosphere didn't feel so . . . off. Like it was a regular room and not a space where Jackson used to berate and hit her. Still, Rodelle steeled herself as she lifted the curtain, letting sunshine into the room through the narrow wavy-glassed window to see better. She spotted the pile of dusty cookbooks propping up a corner of the bed— shades of Jackson, the careless asshole—and yanked them out. The bed thunked to the floor, the sound barely muffled by the homemade rag rug underneath it.

"Everything okay?" Brandon called from the kitchen.

Clutching the books to her chest, Rodelle surveyed the room. Just an ordinary one for New Eden, albeit untidy. The mattress was bare, save for an old blanket and thin sheet.

But it was just a room now. No trace of her dead husband remained.

"Yes," she replied. "I think everything's going to be fine."

CHAPTER THREE

ON THE MORNING of their departure, Rodelle hauled herself out of bed before Brandon could wake her, rising with New Eden's twin suns spilling light across her makeshift bedroom floor. Excitement thrummed through her, an unfamiliar but welcome feeling.

It had been two days since she'd baked doughnuts with Brandon, a memory that even now brought a smile to her lips. They'd been better than she expected, although he had apologized for the ingredient substitutions. The batch she'd shared with Jasmine and Hannah had been appreciated too.

And now, for the first time in longer than she wanted to consider, she was trying something new. Going on an adventure. With Brandon, no less.

She picked up the clean set of clothes she'd left folded on the floorboards the night before, hesitating. Rodelle wanted to take a bath before they set out, one last luxury before they would be at the mercy of the elements. And it *would* be a luxury, because the main house finally had hot water again.

Brandon is still sleeping. Fabric hugged to her chest, she thought about how she'd probably end up waking him, and she didn't want to do that when they had such a trek ahead of them.

He's never been bothered by me being in the house before. Rodelle had thought of the space as Brandon's since he moved in, and before that, Jackson's. She'd just happened to live there. But since the day they'd baked together and he'd talked about renovating, she had started to see the ramshackle house in a different light. It could be a place to truly call her own. She slipped out of the guesthouse and waited at the back door, thinking. It didn't sit in its frame correctly and was splintering at the bottom. Any day now, it would fall off its hinges.

And yet, it felt right that Brandon was here too. Like he belonged here.

So do I. She pushed open the door, wincing at its creaks. Closing it behind her, she tiptoed on bare feet across the kitchen's cracked tile floor. She passed the living room, where Brandon slept on the ancient couch, its fabric mended so many times that the patches swallowed up whatever its original color was. A threadbare sheet was draped over his hips while he slept, his long body sprawled over the couch, legs dangling over the edge. The metal implants and ports embedded in his skin glowed dully in the dim light. She wished he had taken her offer of sleeping in her bed.

The living room window was cracked but otherwise intact, a thin white curtain pinned above it. Early morning sunlight filtered through the cloth, casting itself on Brandon's magnificent form. Rodelle's breath caught, and she realized she was staring.

Definitely rude.

She hurried through the living room as quickly and

quietly as she could, grateful that the rag rug under her feet muffled her steps. Heat crept up her cheeks, and she knew she had to be blushing furiously. Why the hell did that happen? It was embarrassing. Brandon was her *friend.*

Down a short hallway off the living room, there was a bedroom to her left, the bathroom to her right. Rodelle let herself into the latter, closing the door behind her. A bathtub in the middle of the room, set into the floor, had a cold-water hand pump installed at the end closest to the door. Next to it, a slightly more modern, automatic hot-water faucet that, until a few weeks ago, had been useless. Rodelle plugged the tub, then turned on the hot water. She pumped some cold, then waited until it was full before sinking in.

A sigh of contentment escaped her. She would never, ever take hot water for granted again. Or any of the other wonderful things the cyborgs brought or did to help restore New Eden's settlement.

Rodelle lay in the steaming water until she heard Brandon move, hauling himself off the couch, the springs under him rusting and squeaky. Footsteps sounded as he walked to the kitchen, and she idly wondered if he had decided on coffee or tea today. She washed her hair and body with sap soap made by Jasmine, guessing he'd probably want to bathe while he still had the chance.

I wonder if he sleeps naked? His legs had been bare, after all.

Light steam still hung in the air when she left the bathroom, pleasantly fragranced by the soap. Rodelle found Brandon sitting on the couch, sheet still in his lap, a homemade mug in his hand. His short, dark hair stuck up at all angles around his head. "Good morning."

Something quivered in Rodelle's belly at the sight of his grin, as it usually did when he sent a smile her way. The sensation had definitely been stronger as of late. She tried not to show that she was flustered. "Good morning. Are you ready for the trip?"

"I will be soon, right after I take a bath."

"Good choice. I'm guessing there won't be much in the way of amenities in the north."

"If what our preliminary scans show are accurate, no. I don't expect the ocean in that part of the continent to be warm enough to swim or bathe in." He paused, as if considering what little he knew of that part of New Eden. "The water's probably drinkable, but that's it."

"I wish I could read your reports."

Brandon tapped his head. "If I could figure out a way to project the data on your wall like a film, I'd do it."

Rodelle had read about films but never seen one. She doubted she ever would. "That seems like something that would require extensive brain surgery." The thought of Rhys, Hannah's cyborg partner, being put under after one of his brain components failed was enough to make her shudder. She hadn't even been on board the ship when his emergency surgery occurred. Instead, she'd heard about it secondhand from Jasmine, who had been there for Hannah's sake.

"To be honest, I don't understand everything in our data," Brandon continued. "I've had to download notes from the others who have a better understanding of geology, physics, pretty much everything that isn't cooking-related."

"I wish you wouldn't dismiss that," Rodelle said.

"What, my cooking? It's not a big deal in the grand scheme of things."

"Food is sort of important for living, you know."

He shrugged. Rodelle tried not to notice how the muscles in his shoulders bunched when she did so. *Oh, God above, he's still mostly naked.* She'd been doing so well at keeping herself from remembering that. His dark blue eyes fixed on hers. "I prefer to see it as a pleasure, rather than a chore."

She nearly asked him what else he considered pleasures before stopping herself in time. "So are hot baths," she blurted out instead, then immediately felt like an idiot.

Brandon regarded her thoughtfully for a few seconds. She had no idea what he was thinking as a small smile played out on his lips. "So they are. As are beds and couches, anything that isn't a pod where I have to sleep standing up."

Oh, God, he'd mentioned beds. Had his voice taken on a huskier note, or was it Rodelle's imagination? "I'd guess so. You don't have to sleep on the couch. You can take my bed."

There was that inscrutable look on his face again. Her own heated at the thought of him there.

He drained his cup. "I'll take that," Rodelle offered. He handed it over, the pottery still warm from his tea.

Rising, the sheet still wrapped around his waist, he headed for the bathroom. "I may take you up on that offer another time," he said over his shoulder, closing the door behind him.

Her free hand flew to her mouth. An odd half-squeak, half-giggle escaped her, and she hoped he hadn't heard it.

"We're going on a mission," she murmured to herself. She washed out his mug, then boiled some water for coffee. "We're *friends*. We're roommates. I'm too old for him, anyway."

They were common refrains she told herself since he'd moved in, but it was getting more difficult to believe them.

———

ACCORDING to Brandon's internal chronometer, it was half past seven when he and Rodelle walked to the untended field where the cyborgs' ship waited. A few cyborgs were leaving for another off-world supply run, and a smaller group would be traveling to the north. Backpacks had been hauled out of storage and were now loaded with dehydrated food, water, and sleep sacks. Where the packs had come from, Brandon couldn't say. They'd been on board the ship since before he was hatched in the cloning tank.

As he slung the pack over his shoulders, he thought about the dismal excuses for food packed away in them and sighed. He'd been spoiled living on New Eden, having so much time to play around with ingredients. He should have thought to save a few doughnuts for the trip.

He glanced at Rodelle, now pulling her long, dark-blonde braid out from under the pack strapped across her shoulders. She adjusted its straps. "Is it too heavy for you?" he asked quietly.

She shook her head. "It's fine."

"If it gets too heavy, let me know."

"Will do."

"We can't leave yet," CW44 announced. He eyed Rodelle with a critical eye. Brandon felt himself bristle at his silent reproach. "Rodelle, I'm sorry, you can't go trampling over rocks and through caves in sandals." He looked over his shoulder at a cyborg striding up the ship's airlock ramp. "Do we have any suitable footwear in storage that will fit Mrs. Lansing?"

"Just Rodelle."

"Anything that will fit Rodelle?" CW44 amended.

"Doubtful. We have enough fuel to run the replicator, if you want to make something."

Brandon inclined his head at the ship. "How do you feel about a new pair of shoes?"

Her face lit up. "Pretty good." She shrugged off the pack and dropped it in the grass. Relief flashed over her face for a split second, too fast for anyone without cybernetic senses to notice. Brandon suspected he'd have to carry at least some of its contents for the trip, an easy enough feat for him.

He left his in the grass, too, then led her into the belly of the ship. There was a replicator unit in the storage room off the starboard cargo bay, which he made a beeline for. "Have you been aboard the ship before?"

"A couple of times, just to look around. I didn't see much of it."

"I'll have to take you on a proper tour someday, boring as it is. Can I borrow your sandals?"

She blinked. "They won't fit you."

He smiled. She did have a wry sense of humor. "When we're aboard."

"Sure." There was a note of curiosity in her voice, one he loved to hear. It was so much fun to delight her.

And make her flustered. He couldn't forget how she'd blushed so prettily earlier in the morning, when he'd talked about baths and beds. It was good to see that haunted look leave her face. Brandon's ability to read facial expressions was better than most of the other cyborgs, likely because his original hadn't had his emotions beaten out of him in the military. The way that she looked stricken whenever her late husband was brought up was concerning. He'd wondered what the hell Jackson Lansing had done to her during their marriage to make her look like that.

The storage room replicator took a few seconds to sputter to life, its screens blinking before casting a sickly glow across the room. "Can I get your sandals now?" he asked.

Without taking fascinated eyes off the machine, she slipped them off her feet. They were obviously homemade, raw cowhide leather with braided straps. "Will I get them back?"

"Of course. I just need to know what size to make them." Brandon brought up a spec request on the machine and tapped a few commands on one of the screens.

"Can you interface your brain with that?"

"Yeah, but I don't like to."

"What about the shared broadcast mind link all of you had?"

Brandon picked out a waterproof material for the shoes' construction. "I don't miss it now that we're living here. I like being a regular human." He rolled up his shirt sleeve to reveal a port in his wrist. "Except for these."

"Do they bother you?"

He shrugged. "Not really. They're part of who I am. I've always had them. I've had flashbacks from my original, and I can see his arms covered in artwork, so I think he had some tattoos. Real old world shit. If I can figure out a way to do them myself, I think I'd like to try my hand at body artwork, something to match the metal." As much of a careless and irresponsible bastard as he suspected Brayden Emerson was, the man had had good taste in body art. Entire scenes from unspoiled nature had been inked into his arms.

The replicator made a grinding noise. "It's working," he reported.

"Now what happens?"

"We wait for the comp to construct shoes better suited to long-distance walking, then try them on. Then we can set out."

"I feel like an idiot for not considering footwear before."

"Why?" The machine groaned in protest. Brandon pounded it with the side of his fist until it stopped. "Sorry, this one's old and probably running low on material. Why would you feel stupid for not thinking about shoes?"

"I just do, is all. Thank you for making a new pair." She gave him a shy smile.

"No thanks necessary, but you're welcome. Thank *you* for being impressed by our fifty-year-old technology." The machine let out a final stutter that reverberated through the deck, then beeped. "I think your shoes are done." He pulled back a screen to reveal the unit's dispenser. A pair of brown imitation naroki-skin boots waited inside, looking absurdly small compared to the footwear worn by the cyborgs. He held them out to her.

Rodelle looked at them for a few seconds, delight evident in her expression as she turned them over in her hands. "Thank you!"

Warmth spread through him at her reaction. "How do they fit?"

She tried them on, adjusting their straps, and took a couple of experimental steps around the storage room. "Perfectly." She looked around the storage room in wonder, as if the old weapons lockers filled with outdated equipment should be impressive. Her gaze landed on him, a dreamy expression on her face. And damn, if that didn't make him feel good.

She grabbed his hand, surprising him. Her touch was electric, sending sparks up his arm. "Are you ready to go?"

———

THE GROUP HEADED for the north included Brandon, Rodelle, and CW44. "This is disappointing," Rodelle said. She fiddled with the straps on her pack. God above, but it was heavy.

"Should I find that insulting?" CW44 asked.

Brandon looked away, but not before he could hide his smile.

"No, we should be disappointed that no one else from New Eden wanted to go," Rodelle replied.

"This could end up being a total waste of time, so I'm not surprised that hardly anyone was jumping up and down offering to walk for days," CW44 replied. He cast a critical eye on Rodelle. "Are you sure you're going to be able to handle that backpack? Brandon and I can split it up."

Brandon nodded enthusiastically.

Rodelle shook her head. "No, I want to at least try."

"Suit yourself. If it gets too heavy, let us know."

"It won't." She hoped she was telling the truth.

The cyborgs who were leaving with the ship bade them goodbye. Rodelle, Brandon, and CW44 started off, following the overgrown path that led north, where the old comms tower was. The ground vibrated beneath their feet as the ship took off, and Rodelle looked over her shoulder to watch the craft lift gracefully into the sky. Someday, she would get a chance to go off-world aboard it.

But not before she had a chance to explore the unknown parts of her own planet. Excitement thrummed in her at the prospect. She walked alongside Brandon, with CW44 on Brandon's other side, until they reached the comms tower about half a kilometer away.

From here, they could turn left and reach the waterfalls and a wooded area where Rodelle and so many others whiled away the time. West of the waterfalls was the hydroelectric plant, newly restored and fully functioning. It felt odd, continuing north when the path stopped. She held back for a few seconds, looking back at the New Eden settlement. From here, she could see a couple of ramshackle houses and the collapsed medical clinic. They were a stark contrast to the repaired comms tower and power plant. Signs of healing, Rodelle decided.

She didn't realize she was staring or that she'd been looking at the only place she'd ever called home until CW44 cleared his throat. "Sorry," she muttered.

"It's fine," Brandon said, sending a warning look CW44's way. The other cyborg's perpetually stoic expression remained unchanged. "I get it. I felt the same way when we had to leave our asteroid."

"Why?" CW44 deadpanned.

"Because it was the closest thing we had to a home. And Rodelle's leaving hers for the first time," Brandon replied. To Rodelle, he added, "Am I right?"

"Yes," she replied. "And I know you probably think it's weird that hardly anyone has left to explore, but what would we have done if someone returned injured, if they returned at all?" She arched a brow at CW44, who merely blinked in response. "And, as you pointed out this morning, we didn't exactly have the appropriate exploring gear." She looked down at her new boots, wiggling her toes in them. They had to be the most comfortable things she'd ever worn.

"Sensory arrays are necessary on a trip like this," CW44 admitted.

"Are they in your cybernetics?"

"Yes, and we have some handheld equipment. The northernmost part of the landmass has an extensive cave network. If there's any evidence of the original settlers being pirates or smugglers, it'll be easier and safer to find hiding spots."

"This is what I mean. This *is* fascinating," Rodelle insisted. "I still can't believe no one else wanted to go with us."

"I thought Hannah would want to go at least," Brandon said.

"Can we talk and walk at the same time?" CW44 asked.

Rodelle and Brandon obediently picked up the pace, keeping up with CW44's brisk walk. At least, she could for now. The new shoes certainly helped. She wasn't sure she could keep it up all day and might have to accept CW44's offer to take some of her supplies.

They walked through brush that reached Rodelle's waist in some spots, overgrown native grass, mixed with dandelions that dotted most of New Eden's landscape. "I'm not surprised Hannah didn't want to go," Rodelle said.

"She's your leader. She's needed at the settlement," CW44 replied.

"No, it's not just that. One of her friends—her old boyfriend, I guess—started off for the north about five years ago and never returned."

"Shit," said Brandon in surprise, just as CW44 said, "Are we expected to bring back his body for a proper burial?"

"Oh, God, I hope not," Rodelle said. Her stomach clenched at the possibility that she might have to see James Thierry's dead body. Would there even be one left, if they came across it? Her rudimentary knowledge of the planet's geography told her that the climate was almost as mild as it was in the south. Could human remains last five years in the open air?

She didn't realize she had spoken her last thought aloud until CW44 said, "Possibly, especially since New Eden doesn't have any predators."

No predators anymore, Rodelle thought. *Not since Jackson was buried.* Thankfully, she managed to keep herself from voicing it.

"I'm not entirely certain we'll find answers in the north, but I'm curious enough that it's worth a shot," CW44 said. "I definitely don't believe the first settlers were the tech-avoidant fanatics they pretended to be. The choice of this planet as a hideaway is simply too perfect, too convenient, for people to find without sophisticated equipment."

"Plus, there's the comms tower's destruction," Brandon added. The comms tower was recently discovered not to be deliberately destroyed so much as taken apart for future reconstruction.

"I'm not questioning that our great-great-whatever grandparents might not have been the well-intentioned cultists they pretended to be," Rodelle said. "I'm questioning why more New Edeners wouldn't want to check this out for themselves, now that we can do this safely." She looked up at Brandon, then at CW44. "This *is* safe for us, right?"

"We have enhanced healing abilities, so Brandon and I are fine," CW44 replied.

"CW44 has medical training, and we have supplies in case anything happens to you," Brandon added, shooting another warning look at CW44.

If the other cyborg was fazed by it, he didn't let on. "Don't eat anything that we haven't analyzed first."

"I hadn't planned on it. I was looking forward to meals of dehydrated vegetable cubes," Rodelle replied brightly. Brandon gave a low groan of distaste.

"We still have a few hours before a scheduled meal break where we get to enjoy food in cube form, and I'd like to cover as much ground as possible," CW44 said. With pointed looks at Brandon and Rodelle, he said, "Pick up the pace."

She wasn't entirely sure if he was joking or not. Like Rhys, CW44 wasn't a cyborg who seemed to have much of a sense of humor. The brush they were walking into was growing thicker, twigs scraping at her exposed skin. She kept up, pushing branches and grass out of the way, hoping there would be a clearing soon.

Rodelle glanced at Brandon, who gave her an easy smile. She returned it. He leaned over to whisper in her ear, "If you get tired, tell me." He reached out to squeeze her hand.

"I don't plan on getting tired, but if I do, I'll tell you." She squeezed back.

He led her around a large rock straight ahead. As they continued to walk, branches and leaves catching in their hair, she noticed Brandon didn't let go of her.

CHAPTER FOUR

CW44 BROKE through Brandon's thoughts, startling him. *Is this trip going to be like the first supply run?*

Brandon didn't need to ask for details. He'd been aboard the ship for that run too. Still, he played dumb. *What are you talking about?*

CW44 arched a brow in Brandon's direction. Brandon glanced at Rodelle, wanting to see if she noticed their silent exchange, but she was staring straight ahead. The brush had given way to long, blue-green grass fronds, much easier to navigate than the tangle of branches they'd fought through for the first two-and-a-half hours of walking. *In the parlance of our fellow New Edeners, are you two going to make things weird?* CW44 asked.

I hadn't planned on it. Brandon gave his best stern look to CW44. *Stop talking to me over the link. It's rude when unenhanced people are here.* He felt off describing Rodelle as "unenhanced." It felt disrespectful, somehow, like she was less important than someone with a cybernetic heart. *What are we doing that makes you think that, anyway?*

You were holding hands. CW44 didn't need to speak the words to sound so perplexed.

Yeah, for about five minutes, two hours and fourteen minutes ago. The branches were rough. We're friends. Brandon's feelings for Rodelle weren't entirely platonic, but that wasn't something he was sure she wanted to explore. She'd made it clear that she wasn't looking for anything more from him or anyone.

I really need both of you to understand that this isn't a sightseeing trip. We have to confirm if there's stolen tech or supplies or something in the north, see if it's as truly uninhabitable as the original settlers claimed, and go home.

You've developed a taste for planetside comforts, Brandon remarked, barely suppressing a smile.

Yes. I really hate nutrition cubes and sleeping on the ground.

You've never slept on the ground before in your current iteration.

I've never had a stomach virus either, and I don't have to have one to know that I'll hate it. I'm certain my original and previous clones despised sleeping outside too.

"Why are you two talking without me?" Rodelle asked. Her voice carried over the field of blue-green fronds. Odd, since the altitude hadn't changed during their trek. Maybe Brandon just wasn't used to the outdoors.

"CW44 wants to get there and get home as fast as we can," Brandon said.

She didn't look convinced but didn't press the issue. She pulled out a long frond, inspecting it as they walked through it. "Can you tell what this is? We don't have this kind of grass at the settlement."

"I'd have to run an analysis on the ship to tell for sure," CW44 replied. "I suspect the original settlers brought a lot of flora species native to your old world, and that invaded New Eden's existing ecosystem. I doubt dandelions, tall fescue, or ryegrass spontaneously started growing in the settlement. I doubt it even exists anywhere else in the galaxy now."

"I guess that's why we've had hay and wine," she replied. "We aren't walking through a toxic field, are we?"

"Our sensors would have alerted us," Brandon assured her. Her smile of acknowledgement bolstered his spirit.

She collected a few more fronds, braiding them as they walked. "Do you think these could be used for sunhats or something? Jasmine's always looking for new materials to make clothing with." She tested the braid's strength, easily pulling it apart. With a frown, Rodelle tossed it away.

"I'm unfamiliar with the tensile strength needed to produce garments from plants, so she would have to experiment with them." CW44 pulled out a couple of long pieces and inspected them, mild curiosity on his face, before dropping them at his feet.

A light breeze picked up, sending the tall blue-green fronds swaying. It had the odd effect of an ocean, or an imitation of an ocean, created by someone who had never seen one before. Come to think of it, Brandon hadn't seen an ocean in his life before he came to New Eden, nor had his flashbacks ever included large bodies of water. Wherever his original had been from, it was noisy and polluted, as far removed from nature as could be.

"There aren't any trees," Rodelle commented.

Brandon and CW44 exchanged a look. The other cyborg looked surprised that he hadn't made that observation.

"Do you think the trees in the settlement are native to New Eden?" she asked.

"Doubtful. Based on the scans our ship took, there are probably small patches of forest closer to the northernmost part of the continent, but I expect them to be of a different species," CW44 replied.

It irked Brandon that he was mostly at a loss when it came to answering Rodelle's questions. *Can you send me all of your scan data?* he silently asked.

I thought you didn't want to use our link?

For fuck's sake, just throw me a bone, here.

CW44 didn't reply, only uploaded a directory. Brandon blinked at the impact. He wasn't used to downloading things in his head, preferring to pull up data and files on ship comps like a normal humanoid.

Will you have time to unpack all that before she asks about soil? CW44 asked.

Brandon didn't reply. Besides, soil quality was Hannah Forsyth's domain.

"Are you talking without me again? That's rude," Rodelle said.

"No, I just asked for his saved data. He had files I didn't." Brandon opened the directory. Information sprawled into his brain, so much that he nearly stumbled over the grass. It was like watching a soufflé expand in rapid time, filling his head.

He blinked in surprise. He'd never made a soufflé as his current iteration. He had the feeling that, if presented with separated eggs, cow's milk, and butter, he could probably figure it out without a recipe. There was still flour in Rodelle's kitchen. The agri-center was now home to calves, albeit cloned calves. Maybe when they got a little older, he could help himself to some of their milk, and . . .

"Brandon, you're spacing out," Rodelle announced.

Damn it, he was supposed to be thinking about the northern New Eden landscape, not cuisine. "Sorry, I was thinking."

"About what?"

"Soufflés."

"What the hell is a soufflé?" CW44 asked.

"It's a puffy chicken-egg-based dish." He could picture it in his mind. Brayden had made soufflés in his culinary career.

CW44 eyed him suspiciously. "Are you having flashbacks?"

"Yes." Rodelle sucked in a harsh breath. "It isn't anything serious," he quickly added. "This isn't like Rhys's situation. We all have them from time to time, and mine aren't traumatic. They're mostly of food and tattoos."

To Rodelle, CW44 said, "Did you know that Brandon's original was probably a cook or a chef in need of funds?"

"I didn't know about the funds part," Rodelle said.

"That's the theory." Brandon looked over the sea of grass. It felt endless. How could he already be bored of the landscape? He accessed CW44's files, needing to know if the environment would change anytime soon. A topographical map of the landmass appeared in his mind, projecting itself in his vision. It was bisected with the view ahead of him. Three dots appeared, slowly moving, that represented him, Rodelle, and CW44. According to it, they had another 21.4 kilometers of grass to walk through before they reached a creek of moving water. He blinked to clear away the map's image.

"Hannah said that your originals were in it for the money," Rodelle said shyly, as if she was worried about offending them.

"It's the best reason any of us can think of as to why a restaurant cook would end up in a cyborg program. I think most of the others were military or special ops, that kind of thing. I don't think about it that much," Brandon said.

CW44's lips were pursed in a straight line, as if the mention of financial motivation was a sore spot. It probably was, although the other cyborg tended to keep to himself. Brandon wondered what, if any, flashbacks he might have.

When he thought about cooking and restaurants, he thought about food, and his internal chronometer reminded him that it was just past noon. While Brandon and CW44 could function on reserved energy for hours, Rodelle couldn't. She was still keeping up with their pace, but he could see half-moons forming under her eyes and sweat beading on her face under her wide-brimmed hat woven from straw. "Are you hungry?" he asked.

"Yes." Her response was automatic.

"Even for bland nutrition cubes?"

"I'm hungry enough that they sound almost good."

Brandon grinned. Beneath her perpetual tan, Rodelle blushed. He looked around the field, noting that there wasn't a single clearing in sight. "I suppose here is as good a spot as any to set up a picnic."

With inhuman speed, CW44 started clearing away some of the grass fronds. Brandon helped, noting Rodelle's gasp of surprise. "That works," Rodelle commented, impressed at the small clearing.

They settled in it, surrounded by grass that stretched above their heads. A look of relief crossed Rodelle's face as she shucked off her pack. She rubbed the spot where her left shoulder met her neck. Brandon reached for her, hand hovering over the area. "Can I?" he asked.

Her pupils dilated briefly, so quickly that, if he didn't have enhanced vision, he would have missed it. He massaged the sore spot, the sensors in his fingertips alerting him to mild strain. "I'm taking some of the stuff in your pack," he announced.

"I'm fine."

"Your neck is sore." His fingers found a tender spot

and lightly pressed into it. Her eyes slipped closed and her breath caught, a moan of pleasure escaping her.

The sound had every cell in Brandon's body on alert. Visions of ways to get her to do it again filled his mind, and he stilled as he imagined what she would look like underneath him, her long legs twined around his body . . .

Rodelle straightened, and his hand fell away. CW44 arched an eyebrow at him in a wordless judgment. "If you're still hungry, I rehydrated some cubes," he said, holding up a square-shaped carton. Its top was open, revealing a dismal-looking, damp mush of vegetable and protein powder. Two others were opened, waiting on the ground.

"I'm only saying *thank you* to be polite," Brandon said, picking up a carton. He snapped off a spork from the side. Rodelle did the same, then cautiously sniffed the carton's contents.

With a sigh, Brandon took a bite. *Fuck me, this is worse than I remember.*

It was remarkable how quickly he'd adapted to life on New Eden. Just a few months ago, he would have sucked it up and gone on a multi-day trek through the uninhabited, unexplored part of a backwater planet without a single complaint. It took far less time to adapt to living like a regular human than he ever would have thought. The idea that his original hadn't been a military man grew stronger the longer he lived here. He truly wasn't cut out for uniforms, marching, and ass kicking.

Neither was Rodelle. She deserved to have a nice life, free from struggles and pain, free from whatever shit Jackson had put her through. Part of him ached to ask her what had happened between them, what he'd done to put that haunted look on her face, why she flinched at the smallest noise whenever she was in the main house. Those weren't the motions of a grieving widow; they were the reactions of a traumatized woman who wasn't ready to re-assemble her life. It galled Brandon to no end that no one else, cyborg or not, seemed to see that.

"Did you see the creek on the map?" CW44 asked, snapping him out of his daydreams.

"Yeah. Do you think we could make it by late after-noon, set up camp for the night?" Out of the corner of his eye, he noticed Rodelle perk up at the mention of camping. He wasn't sure why, since she'd been living in a situation that was barely a half-step up from camping for years.

"We could make it to the north altogether by nightfall if we ran," CW44 pointed out.

"*You* could make it to the north by nightfall if you ran," Brandon returned.

"So could you."

Brandon leaned back on the ground. Short blades of grass poked his palms, setting off his sensors. "No way. I'm getting soft in my time planetside. I *like* getting soft."

CW44 looked at him as if he'd grown a second head. Brandon grinned in response.

"Is my tagging along really going to be a problem?" Rodelle asked in a small voice. "I can go back to the settle-ment if I'm going to slow you down."

Alarm flared through Brandon at the suggestion. "No! We've been traveling for over half a day already!"

"I can find my way back, I'm sure."

"Absolutely not. Rhys asked for volunteers, and you offered. You're welcome to travel with us. If speed is what my friend here is concerned about, I will carry you while we run," Brandon replied firmly. "Soft or not, I can still run a hell of a lot faster than someone unenhanced." He shot a warning look at CW44, who merely blinked in response.

"Good point," the other cyborg finally replied. "My apologies for any offense caused."

"None taken. I'd like for us to stay civil during this trip," Rodelle replied. She looked at the ground, tiny blue-green shoots sprouting around them. "The grass is growing again!"

"My sensors picked that up right away," CW44 said. "The foliage here is exceptionally fast-growing, but it isn't toxic or poisonous."

"I guess that's why the original settlers brought their own grass seeds," Rodelle said.

"Yes. It's as if they studied this planet carefully before they settled here. Not exactly the hallmarks of people who hated technology." CW44 picked a tiny frond and examined it, peering at it to activate his ocular enhancements.

"Does that mean you're fully on board with seeing what's in the north?" Brandon couldn't resist asking.

CW44 turned an affronted gaze on him. His eyes had taken on a metallic, silvery hue, a sure sign that he was still using his enhancements. "Of course, I'm on board. I've been on board with everything since we intercepted Hannah's SOS. I'm curious, is all. I'm hoping that our curiosity isn't misplaced and this trip isn't a waste of time."

"It won't be a waste of time at all," Rodelle protested. "At least, not for me. I've never been this far away from the settlement in my life. Even if there isn't anything in the north, at least I can say I made it there and back. I'll have finally seen something other than a bunch of falling-down buildings." She looked wistfully at the grass surrounding them. "I wish I'd thought to ask Jasmine if I could take some of the paper and pencils she brought back with her from the waystation before we left. I'd love to try drawing what we see." She plucked a long blade of grass from behind her and rolled it between her fingers.

"We could always come back. This field isn't that far from the settlement, in the grand scheme of things," Brandon replied. He finished the last of his nutrition cube, not sorry to know that he wouldn't get another for a few hours yet. Rodelle picked at hers, but after an encouraging look from Brandon, finished it. She needed her strength for the journey ahead.

CW44 buried the remains of the cubes' packaging in the dirt, where it would quickly decompose. Judging by the way the grass was re-growing, the foliage didn't need the nutrients. "Onward," he said gruffly, rising.

Brandon rose, then held out a hand to help Rodelle up. "Onward."

———

RODELLE WAS GETTING DIZZY.

She was hydrated, thanks to regular water breaks and Brandon's urging her to drink, and she wasn't hungry. The pack strapped to her shoulders was heavier than she was used to, but still bearable. Her sunhat protected her from the rays of the twin suns overhead, which now looked like they were about to start setting. No, it was the never-ending fields of grass that were doing her in, making her eyes play tricks on her. Her initial delight at a change of scenery had given way to an odd feeling she couldn't immediately put a name to.

Unsettling, she decided. It crept up her spine, spreading outward, until her muscles stiffened, hands gripping her pack's straps so tightly that her knuckles turned white. Rodelle had once read about the uncanny valley theory, and as she looked over the flat landscape covered in rolling fields, the color a weird imitation of the grass she was used to at the settlement, she wondered if this was what the theory's researchers were thinking about. A weird simulation that didn't quite hit the mark on reality.

She sneaked a glance at Brandon, who had been staring ahead, looking bored. Why hadn't she ever felt that uncanny sense when she looked at him or the other cyborgs? Just as quickly, she answered herself. *They are still real humans, albeit ones with extra features.* Their eyes occasionally went blank or silvery as they accessed files in their bodies, and the skin was studded with metallic bits and ports, but none of those things were unnerving.

She lost track of time as they strode along, grass lightly waving against their legs. It was getting cooler, although Rodelle had no idea if it was because of the time of day or the area's geography. How far away from the settlement were they, anyway?

"How big is New Eden?" she asked.

CW44 jumped at the sound of her voice, as if he'd been lost in thought. "Are you referring to the planetary size or the landmass?"

"The landmass."

"Are you looking for exact dimensions or an estimate?"

"An estimate is fine."

"Two hundred and twenty square kilometers, approximately. It, like the planet itself, is small," CW44 replied.

"It feels big to me." Rodelle dragged her hand through the grass. Her shoulders and back ached, but she would be damned before she would ask either cyborg for help. She could *do* this. At least, she still appeared to be keeping up with Brandon and CW44.

"The creek should be half a kilometer away," Brandon reported, finally speaking.

"I'm surprised you noticed it," CW44 replied.

"Just because I don't have the military background you and the others do, doesn't mean I can't hear water when it's this close." Brandon paused. CW44 and Rodelle halted in their tracks, watching as Brandon tilted his head to the side. "It doesn't sound like a creek."

Now it was CW44's turn to listen. "It sounds like running water, which is what one would expect to find in a creek."

"Yeah, but like there's a hell of a lot *more* running water than you would expect in a creek."

"We've never seen a creek before," CW44 pointed out.

"Blame it on flashbacks from my original, I don't know. Whatever's ahead of us is not a little creek we can just hop over." Brandon's lips thinned. "There's an automatic raft in our supplies, isn't there?"

"Yes, large enough for the three of us. It's in my pack."

Despite the tense tone the conversation had taken, Rodelle was curious about the automatic raft. She didn't speak, waiting to hear what the others wanted to do about crossing a creek that might not be a creek.

"We might have to use that raft. If we do, it might be best to make camp beside the creek and pick up tomorrow morning. It's going to be dark soon, and I don't want to try to navigate unfamiliar waters until then." Brandon gave a wry look to Rodelle. "Of course, it's not like any of us have any experience with rafting, but I'd rather not chance it."

"It's not dark. The suns are still out," Rodelle protested. The shadows cast by them were longer, but they hadn't set yet. They had at least an hour before they did.

"I agree. If we get to the creek and we can cross it safely, we should do that," CW44 replied. "We're wasting daylight."

Brandon gave them a dubious look. "You can hear the water, can't you? It doesn't sound like a creek."

They started walking again, Rodelle and CW44 on

either side of Brandon. "Are you suggesting we go back already?" CW44 asked.

"We've come this far," Rodelle added.

"I'm just—" Brandon looked up at the sky, as if it would give him answers. "Maybe we should have waited until we had a chance to take better preliminary scans. You and I will be fine." He glanced at the other cyborg. "It's Rodelle I'm worried about."

Warmth spread through her at his words, in a way that had nothing to do with New Eden's perpetual heat. "I wouldn't have tagged along if you thought this would be dangerous."

"I was thinking about predators," Brandon said.

"Not about the caves themselves?" CW44 muttered.

"We have equipment to analyze the caves first."

"Why didn't you analyze the rest of the landmass before we set out?" Rodelle asked.

"We don't have the tech do that kind of wide-range planetary scan. Northern landmass analysis would have to be done a lot closer to it. We'd probably have to land the ship in the area to do that," Brandon explained. "The information we do have isn't terribly specific. We've always been so focused on the settlement in the south instead."

"Well, yeah, that's where the people are," Rodelle said. She shifted her pack's straps. Creek or not, she was looking forward to settling down for the night and taking off the damn thing.

"Right." Brandon didn't meet her eyes, instead keeping his gaze straight ahead. A frisson of unease threaded through Rodelle at his expression. She'd never seen him so tense before.

None of them spoke until they reached the creek. The grass gave way to a thin shore, sparsely populated with sagging fronds and pebbles. Ahead of them, water rushed past, the speed reminding Rodelle of the waterfalls near the hydroelectric plant. It definitely wasn't the meandering stream she had seen in pictures, with a gentle trickle of water slipping by. Her heart sank.

"That's really more of a river, isn't it." Brandon's voice was flat.

"How deep do you think it is?" Rodelle asked cautiously. She peered over the strip of shore. She guessed the other side was about three meters away, a doable distance if the water wasn't rushing as fast as it was. She could see a pebbled bottom from where she stood, but had no idea how deep it was farther away from the shore. "Are there any insects in there?"

Brandon knelt next to the river and put out a hand in the water. His eyes took on a metallic hue as he analyzed the water. "It's approximately a meter deep at this point, moving at six kilometers an hour," he reported.

Optimism rose in Rodelle. "That's not too bad."

"Six kilometers an hour can be faster than you expect. I also can't tell how deep it is at other points." He stood and looked to either side, gauging Rodelle's and CW44's reactions. "What do you two think?"

"I say we take off our shoes and cross it." Rodelle bent over a little to unfasten one of her boots, swaying to the side from the weight of her pack.

"There aren't any lifeforms in it I could pick up, other than some foliage. The water's fresh and unpolluted, so nothing to worry about on that front." There was still a note of unease in Brandon's voice, something that concerned Rodelle. When she looked at CW44, he wore his usual unreadable expression. She knew him well enough to know that he would speak up if he was worried about the river.

CW44's original had been military, she recalled.

Brandon had been a chef. If CW44 wasn't concerned about what lay ahead, then she wouldn't be, either. "I think we should cross now," she announced, then reached for her other boot. Footwear in hand, she took a few steps toward the pebbled shore. Cold water rushed to meet her feet, drawing a gasp from her.

"We have to get across somehow," Brandon said reluctantly. "Are you sure you don't want me to carry you?"

The idea was tempting, alluring, even, but she knew it wouldn't be as romantic as she imagined. Rodelle was capable of walking through fairly shallow water. "A little water never hurt anyone," she said. Meter-deep water meant she might get her shorts wet, hardly anything to fuss over.

Brandon didn't look convinced. He glanced at CW44, as if he expected the other cyborg to voice an opinion. "I'll go first," CW44 volunteered. He adjusted his pack straps and waded into the water, boots and all. He quickly crossed to the other side. "Be careful," he called. "I think there's a drop-off about half a meter from the path I took. I'm not sure how deep it is."

Rodelle was already in the water, fighting back a shriek at the cold water lapping around her ankles. "Rodelle," Brandon said, a low urgency in his voice that she'd never heard before.

He was immediately behind her, still wearing boots and trousers, as CW44 had. The water was definitely moving faster than she thought it would—who would have thought a mere six kilometers an hour would have such an impact? —but she didn't feel like she was in danger, as long as she stepped carefully, and . . .

Her left foot touched a rock, slippery with algae, and she fell in the river, face down. She didn't even have time to scream before her mouth filled with water. When she tried to haul herself up, her hands scrabbled against the rocky, pebbled bottom, fighting the weight of her pack.

A few seconds later, she was jerked out of the water, pack and all, and hoisted over Brandon's shoulder. She sucked in a greedy lungful of air, then coughed. Tears sprang to her eyes.

Brandon set her down on the other side of the river. "Oh, my God! Are you all right?"

"Thank you," she said, voice small.

"No thanks necessary. Are you all right?" he repeated. His eyes had a near-crazed look in them, one she'd never expected to see from him. She tried to remind herself that he was reacting out of concern—that he wasn't shouting at her and his voice had risen in panic—but a primitive part of her brain didn't understand that.

Rodelle was frozen in place, heedless of the chill caused by her soaked clothes. "I'm sorry," she said again, damning the catch in her voice. A million variations of apologies raced through her mind, and she nearly blurted out all of them in an attempt to earn his forgiveness for something that was an accident.

"You didn't do anything wrong," CW44 said sharply. Rodelle couldn't help but flinch at the tone in his voice, even though he wasn't angry.

Brandon's expression had softened. "I'm glad you're okay," he said. "I mean it. Holy shit, but seeing you slip and go under was one of the scariest things I've ever seen." He wrapped his arms around her in a fierce hug. "Let's set up camp."

CHAPTER FIVE

THE LANDSCAPE CHANGED on the other side of the river. The grass was the same blue-green, but it was shorter, sparser than it had been before. Brandon's cybernetics told him it was a related species to the long fronds they'd walked through for hours, although he ignored the analysis that was delivered to his brain. Hills began to rise in the distance, making him glad they'd decided to build camp here. They likely faced another day of walking before they would reach the caves that were beyond the hills. At least that part of the map in his head was accurate.

Rodelle had unloaded her pack, so everything could dry overnight. Most of what she had was cyborg tech, hauled from storage lockers or created in hard goods replicators, designed to quickly dry out. Her things were spread on the grass, forming a barrier around her where she was curled up in her sleep sack. She had pulled it over her head, so only a few wisps of damp, dark blonde hair were visible in the light offered by the stars and twin moons.

All of them had been quiet over their dinner of dehydrated nutrition cubes and strips of cured naroki meat, with Rodelle replying to conversation attempts with one-word answers until Brandon gave up.

The steady flow of the nearby river would have lulled him to sleep if he wasn't so concerned about her reaction to the fall. He had never worried over someone like he did her; as close-lipped as she was about her marriage and life before the cyborgs settled on New Eden, he *knew* something terrible had happened. Something had put that haunted look in her eyes, caused her to flinch at loud noises. He had a pretty good idea that it was her late husband, but if she didn't want to discuss it with him, he wouldn't push the subject.

She stirred, then exhaled in a way that told him she was definitely awake. Brandon stilled, not wanting to scare her or make her anxiety worse. His enhanced senses picked up her movements, from shimmying out of the sleep sack to uncapping a bottle of water and taking a few sips. He was surprised when she tiptoed over to him, indecision on her face. Her voice was a soft whisper. "Brandon? Are you awake?"

His heart pounded against his ribs, sending an alert through his body. "Yes."

"I'm sorry about earlier."

She crouched in the grass next to him. He hauled himself up on his elbows to better look at her. "No," he said. "Don't be sorry. There's no need to apologize. It was an accident."

"You said you should carry me . . ."

"And you're an adult who said she could walk herself, and we thought the river was shallow enough. No one predicted slipping and falling, although we should have, since you were barefoot."

The worry lines around her eyes smoothed out. "I'm glad you hauled me out. I couldn't get to my feet in time," Rodelle said. "I thought you were . . . I don't know. Not mad. Disappointed."

"I wasn't. I was scared for you." He fumbled for words. "I fell apart, I think. I panicked when I saw you face down in the water, unable to get up. It scared the shit out of me." His heart lurched at the notion of harm coming to her. "I can't imagine a New Eden without you in it."

He hadn't meant to say that. Now that the words were out, he was glad he had.

"Will you carry me over it when we go home?" she asked shyly.

He reached for her hand, stroking the back of it with his thumb. She threaded her fingers through his. "I'll carry you whenever you want."

Rodelle's eyes met his, her gaze then flicking to his lips. His stupid heart's tempo increased as he realized what she wanted to do. The damn thing had no concept of emotional human reactions. He didn't dare move, not wanting to scare her away.

Her kiss landed a little off-center, but Brandon didn't care. His body immediately reacted, every system lighting up in response. He shifted, pulling himself up into a seated position so he could better kiss her back, hands reaching for her hair that he'd ached to run his fingers through since the day she'd said he could stay in her house.

Rodelle's tongue swept into his mouth in a possessive gesture he hadn't expected but welcomed all the same. She inched a little closer, and it would be so easy to pull her against him, pull her on top of him, and . . .

"Are you fucking kidding me, Brandon?" CW44's irritated voice broke the silence. "You promised me this wouldn't turn into another Simon and Darius situation."

Brandon closed his eyes, then drew Rodelle to him, so she could rest her head on his bare chest. Her body vibrated with silent laughter against him. "You really know how to kill the mood," he said.

"We're on a fact-finding mission. There shouldn't be a mood at all. Can't you wait until we get back to the settlement?"

"Wait for what?" Brandon asked innocently.

CW44 made a show of rolling over in his sleep sack, away from Brandon and Rodelle. "Go back to sleep. Do it separately, do it together, I don't care, as long as we get adequate rest."

"We do have auxiliary power supplies, so I'm not sure what he's on about," Brandon murmured into Rodelle's hair.

"What you two do is private, that's all," CW44 said without turning over again.

Rodelle disentangled herself from Brandon's hold. "Can I sleep next to you?" she whispered.

"Of course."

She dragged her sleep sack next to his and crawled back in. What a shame there was only room for one person in each. She rolled on her side to face him. "Good night, Brandon."

He closed the small distance between them to kiss her again. It was far too chaste for his body, which was protesting the loss of contact already. "Good night."

BREAKFAST WAS A QUICK MEAL, eaten as dawn rose across the landscape. Rodelle noted Brandon's brief look of dismay at the food—more bland nutrition cubes and cured naroki strips—was quickly replaced by a heated one in Rodelle's direction.

She felt like giggling as if she was a lovestruck teenager. Rodelle didn't know what had come over her the night before when she kissed him, but she was grateful for the nerves she had managed to summon to do so. She could swear her lips still tingled from their kiss. Shadowy fantasies that she had never voiced in her life came to mind. Ones that had never featured anyone specific before now starred Brandon. Her face heated, and she was sure she had to be blushing furiously. Now, she could hardly wait to return home.

Maybe she would move back into the house, after all. Or tear it down and rebuild, truly make it a space for them, put their personal touches on it.

Am I thinking ahead too quickly? Moving fast had worked for Hannah and Rhys, Jasmine and Simon and Darius. Maybe it would work for her and Brandon too.

Am I too old for him? A few days ago, Rodelle would have said yes, but now she wasn't so sure.

They ate their breakfast in companionable silence, Rodelle wishing she could have a hot cup of coffee to accompany it, when CW44 announced, "I would like to reach the caves today."

"That's forty-four kilometers away," Brandon pointed out. He didn't take his eyes off Rodelle as he spoke.

"Brandon, have you ever heard of a marathon?" CW44 asked.

"I have," Rodelle said.

"I asked Brandon."

Brandon shrugged. "No, what of it?"

"It's an old world long-distance-running race. The traditional distance is forty-two kilometers."

Brandon raised a dark eyebrow. "In a row?"

Rodelle bit back a smile.

"Yes. Athletes would run that course, and competent runners could complete it under four hours." CW44 leaned forward, tenting his fingertips under his chin. "We're giving ourselves, what, eight, ten hours to walk forty-four of them? We're all in decent enough condition to do that, assuming we don't come across any more surprise rivers."

That last remarked pricked Rodelle's pride. "That was low," she muttered.

"It wasn't a dig at your accident," CW44 replied. "I'm pointing out that it isn't unreasonable to walk that much today. We covered almost as much ground yesterday."

"How far away from the settlement are we, anyway?" Rodelle asked.

"Forty point two kilometers," Brandon said.

"Wow." Rodelle set aside her empty food container and leaned back on the grass. "This is the farthest I've ever been in my life. Pretty sad, isn't it?"

"No," said Brandon, just as CW44 said, "Not at all."

"This is the farthest we've been too," Brandon explained. "We lived our entire lives on our terraformed asteroid. Aside from the occasional supply runs, we didn't leave, and the waystations we visited weren't as remote as New Eden."

"How did you terraform the asteroid? Was it already there, or did you wake up in the cloning tanks and decide to build it?" she asked.

Brandon and CW44 exchanged glances. Their eyes didn't go blank, so she knew they weren't communicating with each other. "We woke up in the tanks and built it," Brandon said. "We woke up and knew we needed a new place to live and did it, twenty-eight years ago."

"You've never known any other life, otherwise,"

Rodelle mused. "I want to say that's incredible, but it's not that different from us. Until the quake, anyway." She felt some of her good mood dissipate when she mentioned the quake.

She had to tell Brandon about Jackson, exactly how he'd died. He deserved to know. How the hell would she manage that? She hadn't even told Hannah or Jasmine. The thought of them walking out of her life, the looks of contempt on their faces, when she told them was unbearable to contemplate. She squeezed her eyes shut, willing away an unexpected wave of tears.

"Rodelle? Are you all right?" Brandon's voice was soft, curious. He could probably tell she was upset. He could read her like a book.

She willed away her tears. "I'm okay. Just glad to be here, is all." Opening her eyes, she pasted a smile on her face. She stood and brushed off her shorts. "I'm going to splash some water on my face, if you think the river is clean enough."

"It's fine. Fresh water, the same as the rest of the planet," CW44 replied.

Rodelle walked the short distance to the riverbed. While the grass fronds were sparser than those on the other side, they still gave her a measure of privacy. Kneeling on the pebbled bank, she lowered her face to the water and put her hands in it, the cool temperature an unexpected balm. In a few hours, New Eden would reach its usual searing temperature, although it didn't feel as hot here as it did in the settlement. She pressed damp hands against her cheeks and forehead. At that moment, she missed her bathtub.

She heard Brandon's footfalls before he spoke. "Is this a bad time?" he asked.

"For you? Never."

He kneeled on the riverbank next to her, water soaking into his black trousers. She had never voiced her observation before, but they *really* suited him. "Are you all right? I know I've asked you that before, but it seems like something's still bothering you."

To her surprise, Rodelle was able to answer without a wobble in her voice. Maybe splashing water on her face had given her a little more strength. "I'm really okay. I've just never been so far from home. Thank you for checking in on me, though. I should've just let you carry me across the water."

"You're an adult."

"I'm older than you," she said wryly.

"Ooh, what is it? Six years? Hardly anything to write home about." He sat back on the pebbles and gave her that smile that always made her toes curl. At least he couldn't see that while she was wearing her sturdy, practical cyborg boots. His expression quickly turned serious again. "I'm not mad at all. I'm not Jackson."

Rodelle stared at him in shock. When her eyes met Brandon's, she saw her feelings reflected there, as if he couldn't believe he'd said that, either.

"No," said Rodelle when she found her voice. "You're not him, and thank God for that."

He hesitated. Something in Rodelle twisted in anticipation of being asked a question she didn't want to answer. "I get the impression you two didn't have a great relationship."

Now it was her turn to consider her words, how she was going to reply without breaking down. "We didn't." Rodelle had only recently acknowledged that to Hannah and Jasmine, without going into too many details. "It was arranged. Neither of us wanted to be alone, and it turns out, it's better to be alone than to wish you were."

"He hit you." It wasn't a question.

She took a deep breath, fortifying herself. "Not right away."

"But he worked his way up to it."

"Yes." She finally tore her gaze away from her hands to force herself to look at Brandon. His expression was sad, with an undercurrent of rage to it. A muscle in his jaw ticked. She had the notion that, if Jackson was standing here, the cyborg would tear him limb from limb. Swallowing a hard lump in her throat, she said, "Don't take this personally, but I don't think I want to talk about this right now. Or ever, I don't know."

"You don't have to do anything you don't want to. If you feel like talking, you know where I am."

He looked so sincere, so understanding, that Rodelle nearly blurted out, *"I could have saved him in the quake and didn't."* She stopped herself in time. This was not the right moment to admit that. Instead, she said, "Thank you." She leaned into him, wrapping her arms around his shoulders in a hug she sorely needed.

Brandon's response was immediate. His hold was reassuring, steady, his breath ruffling her hair. She remembered what it was like to kiss him last night, that surge of bravery she'd felt, the long-forgotten flare of desire racing through her veins. More than anything, she felt safe with him.

To her pleasant surprise, he pressed a kiss to the top of her head. "Are you up for more walking now?"

"Is CW44 getting impatient?"

"Not so much that he isn't willing to take a break if you need more time. He's efficient and single-minded, but he gets that life happens sometimes."

Rodelle smiled wryly against his chest, thinking about his reaction the night before to their kiss. "As long as it isn't happening too much while he's trying to rest."

Laughter rumbled in his chest. "He really does have perfect timing." His arms tightened around her. "I'd like to kiss you again sometime."

Heat suffused her body at the husky note his voice had taken. "Me too."

"That was a very welcome surprise, by the way." He pulled away from her, then curled his hand around Rodelle's. Ports in his fingertips lightly scraped against her skin, sending a pleasurable shiver through her. He traced the back of her hand with his thumb. "Let's go."

———

THAT DAY'S hike through the hills was far more difficult than Brandon had anticipated. While it wasn't quite so humid on this part of the landmass, compared to the settlement, the suns' heat still bore down on them uncomfortably, and they took more breaks for water and food than they had the day before.

"We're making better time than I thought we would," CW44 announced when they crested one of the smaller hills of the day.

"Do you think we'll get a chance to explore the cave network by the end of the day?" Rodelle asked. They had walked through a copse of trees earlier, with similar blue-green leaves as the grass, the smooth bark a pale brown, and she'd cut herself a walking stick from one of the branches. The trees registered as unknown species to Brandon's cybernetics, but they weren't poisonous. She said the stick helped her keep up, and if that worked for her, he and CW44 were fine with it.

"It's possible. At least part of it," CW44 replied. "Brandon, are you following along with the map too?"

He hadn't. Brandon preferred to keep his eyes on

Rodelle as she walked ahead of him. He sighed and brought up a visual of the topographic map for the first time since they set off. "Damn," he said in surprise when he saw their progress. "We've covered over twenty-two kilometers today."

"Holy shit!" said Rodelle in excitement. "I think that calls for a water break to celebrate." She shucked off her pack and dug around the front pocket for her water bottle. They'd refilled their supplies at the river before they left, once their scans determined the water was safe to drink. It tasted a little metallic, but was otherwise fine.

Brandon and CW44 followed suit. Rodelle plunked down on a large rock that was half-buried in the sandy soil. "Do you think we could ever move the settlement here?" she asked.

"Why would we do that?" Brandon asked.

"What if there are more earthquakes? Can you tell offhand if this part of the landmass is prone to them?"

Brandon exchanged a glance with CW44. The other cyborg's expression was inscrutable. "Seismic activity surveys would have to be conducted to determine if the north is as susceptible to quakes," Brandon replied. "I'm also unsure if the ecosystem is amenable to the crops you've already cultivated."

Rodelle gestured around their surroundings. Just ahead was another copse of trees, the bark smooth and gray, blue leaves sparse, one of several they'd hiked through today. "Stupid question, but could you tell by looking at the scenery if there's been an earthquake recently?" She tapped the rock under her butt. "This clearly hasn't moved in forever."

CW44's expression turned thoughtful, and he looked at the trees, as if considering Rodelle's hypothesis. "Not a stupid question. I think it's possible that minor quakes could have occurred, but we would have to do more study to be sure. Whatever happens, though, the structures in the settlement will be reinforced to be quake-proof, if they aren't torn down and rebuilt altogether."

That answer seemed to mollify Rodelle. "Good." She took another swallow of water from her canteen, then resealed it. She licked an errant drop off her lower lip, her pink tongue darting out in a way that sent a bolt of desire straight through Brandon. Goddamn it, their kiss last night hadn't been nearly enough.

She rose and adjusted her pack's straps. "Do either of you need to rest for a bit?"

"I'm good," said Brandon, just as CW44 replied, "Cyborgs, remember?"

Eyes shining with excitement, Rodelle pointed up the hill. "Let's go."

She took the lead this time, staying a few meters ahead, improvised walking stick at her side. *This is the most enthusiastic I've ever seen her*, CW44 commented silently.

She's had a rough go of it the last couple of decades. A shower of tiny pebbles slid down the hill under Rodelle's feet.

I do see why you like her so much. She's very sweet. Very concerned for other people.

Jealousy flared in Brandon at his friend's words. Definitely irrational, definitely the human side of him coming out. *She is.*

Don't look like that, Brandon. I'm not out on a mission to wine and dine her away from you. She's a lovely woman, is all. She looks at you like you're a giant star in the sky.

Brandon raised a brow. *I never thought you were the poetic type.*

I'm not. I read that line in an old-world text file. I prefer a more utilitarian metaphor. For example, if someone looked at me like I just repaired their O2 recycler. Clean air is more important than starlight.

That still counts as poetry, coming from you.

CW44 bestowed one of his rare smiles on Brandon. *I'll have to take your word for it.* He pointed ahead, to where Rodelle had reached the peak of this particular hill. *She's making great progress for someone who has been effectively malnourished for years.*

She was a great deal physically stronger now that Brandon was feeding her. All his medical knowledge of humans had been downloaded into his brain circuitry before he woke up in a cloning tank. So, he knew the ideal ratios of protein and carbohydrates to keep a human in their best physical condition. He hadn't bothered to build on his knowledge, preferring to conduct culinary experiments in the galley on the asteroid.

When he thought of culinary experiments, he thought of foraging. Prior to this trip, a part of him had hoped they would come across flora that could be used as seasonings or side dishes, but there had been nothing of the sort so far. New Eden lacked almost everything, aside from fresh water, breathable air, and a few harmless insect species.

Brandon wasn't sure whether it was curiosity or a burning need to just finish this part of the expedition that kept all of them moving at such a brisk clip. They took two more water breaks before the suns turned brilliant orange and gold, a telltale sign of their imminent setting. Before the suns could set, they ascended the final hill, ending in a cliff face over the ocean the topographic map said would be there. Waves gently beat against the cliff below their feet, a sheer drop of six meters to a pebbled beach, by Brandon's estimate. They still had to figure out a way to descend it in order to examine the cave network underneath.

But that wasn't what caught their attention as they gazed at the sight before them. It was the sound of off-key whistling in an unfamiliar song, carried to them by the sea's breeze. Before any of them could congratulate one another on a long trip well-traveled, they spotted the source of the song: a naked man strolling along the beach, without a care in the world.

CHAPTER SIX

RODELLE STARED AT THE BEACH, shocked into silence. She blinked, then rubbed her eyes to reassure herself that she wasn't asleep and dreaming. "What the fuck?" she said, voice barely a whisper.

It had to be James Thierry, missing for, what was it, five years? Five years since he'd started walking to the north, never to return, long presumed dead. Rodelle recognized his distinctive walk, his slight limp from a poorly healed break in his leg when he was little.

"Who the hell is that?" Brandon asked in shock.

She held up her hand to quiet him. "I don't want to scare him. God above only knows what he's been through."

"You know who that is?" Brandon replied, voice a hoarse whisper.

"Yeah. He disappeared years ago." She looked at him again, watching as he half-skipped, half-walked along the beach, occasionally kicking the water. Rodelle pinched the bridge of her nose between two fingers, trying to decide how to handle this. "Okay, I'll go down to the beach first and talk to him. You two will scare the shit out of him."

"But *who* is he?" CW44 pressed.

"James Thierry. He was one of our friends and wandered off one day about five years ago. Look, I'm sure he's going to be pretty messed up after being in the wilderness alone for so long. Let me do this." Rodelle looked around the cliff for the easiest way to descend to the beach.

As she did so, James looked up. Shielding his eyes with his hand, he jumped. "Holy shit!" he yelled.

At least he didn't run away. Rodelle took a couple of cautious steps closer to the cliff's edge. "Hi, James." How did one address a man long thought dead? "How are you?"

"Who is that? The suns are in my eyes."

"Rodelle Lansing."

"Oh! Hey! I wasn't expecting you. Want to come down and say hi?"

Rodelle looked on either side of her, to Brandon and CW44, who both wore matching expressions of shock. "Are you serious?"

God love him, James sounded affronted at her question. "Well, yeah. I wouldn't be a good host if I didn't invite you, would I? It's a long walk here."

"How do we get down?"

James scratched his head. From her vantage point, Rodelle could see that his red-tinged hair was long and tangled. "If you walk to your left for about, I don't know, five or ten meters, the hill starts to shrink, and you can jump down to the beach. I think. I haven't been up there in a while." His head tilted. "Who are your friends? Are they from the settlement? I don't recognize them."

"It's a long story, and I'll tell you when I come down." Brandon and CW44 were already walking in the direction James had indicated. Before she joined them, she called, "We'll be right there."

"Oh, yeah. Sorry, it's been a while since I talked to anyone."

Rodelle quickly caught up with the cyborgs. Her insides shook, and she thought her knees might give way beneath her. "I can't believe it," she said under her breath.

"This part of the landmass must be amenable to humanoid life, after all," CW44 mused.

"That's your takeaway from all this?" Rodelle asked in astonishment.

"Yes. Either that, or your friend is a genius at living off-grid. It's quite remarkable."

"I'm not sure 'genius' is the right word to describe this situation," Brandon said. Rodelle was inclined to agree. She couldn't believe he was alive. Whether his mind was fully intact remained to be seen. She'd never known a hermit before, but she wouldn't have expected one to be so welcoming.

There was a chill in the air when they descended to the beach, sprays of tiny pebbles kicking up under their feet. The ocean lapped at the shore, the sound of waves soothing. Beneath the cliff face were a series of caves, their mouths different sizes and shapes but all huge. Rodelle couldn't even appreciate that they'd finally arrived in the north due to her shock.

James bounded over to them, now wearing an oversized tunic that was threadbare and yellowed from age. It was the same kind of tunic Jasmine had made for everyone at some point. It must have been what he was wearing the day he walked away.

As if he could read her mind, James said, "My shorts fell apart."

"I see." Now that she could get a good look at him, Rodelle could see how much weight he had lost. Never the stout man his late father had been, James was almost gangly, all slender, long limbs and sharp features: cheek-bones that might have been chiseled, a thin blade of a nose. Long reddish-brown hair hung well past his shoulders, roughly braided to keep it off his face. His blue eyes were striking, despite the hollows beneath them, even more so by his deep tan that blended with the freckles scattered across his nose.

"What brings you here? It's been an age." James sounded like he'd just opened the door to his home in the settlement, greeting a visitor. Of course, his home had collapsed in the quake and no one bothered to rebuild it.

She stared at him, agog. It took her a few seconds to regain her voice. "Are you fucking kidding? That's all you have to say? 'It's been an age'?"

James looked at her as though she had sprouted an extra head. "How long has it been? I've lost track." He looked on either side of her. "Who are these two?"

"Five years, and a hell of a lot has happened. They're part of that."

"Oh, yeah. I didn't think either of them looked young enough to be your kids."

"Oh, my God." Rodelle took a deep breath. *He hasn't spoken to another living soul in five years. He has no idea what happened at the settlement.* When she spoke, her voice was measured, clipped, but calm. "This is Brandon and CW44. They're cyborgs." She held her breath, waiting for James's reaction.

His gaze flicked between the two of them, unreadable. "Huh." He was awfully calm for receiving such news. Alarm threaded through Rodelle.

"Cybernetically enhanced humans," CW44 added.

"Yeah, no, I got that. Makes a lot of sense." James shrugged. "I guess if you're cyborgs, then you know what to do with all that stuff in the caves."

———

"WHAT THE FUCK."

Brandon was inclined to agree with CW44's epithet. Led by James into the mouth of the nearest cave, they stood in the center of a room carved out of the rock. Filled with crates holding exactly the kinds of electronic components the original New Edeners had claimed to avoid, the space was the size of the bridge aboard the cyborgs' cruiser. They were old, rusting away from age and disuse, an odd hodgepodge of pieces that Brandon couldn't make sense of.

"Of course, when I came here, I thought, hey, the caves seem like a good place to stay," James said. "Took me a while to figure out how to build a fire out here. There aren't a lot of trees on this part of New Eden, and I wouldn't say I improvised a way to do it, so much as a lot of trial and error. Have you ever tried to build a fire with that weird grass? You can't. It just sort of melts."

"What does fire have to do with the supplies hidden here?" CW44 asked in exasperation.

"I'm getting to that. I found a box in the next cave over that has a lot of, well, I guess they're fire starters? I'm not sure. Anyway, they light up great. This place gets really dark really fast when the suns set. Rodelle, why did you come here?"

James's rapid fire speech and abrupt change of subject had Brandon's head proverbially swimming. Rodelle was looking through one of the boxes in wonder, pulling out a heating coil that had to be hundreds of years old. "This is exactly why we came here," she said.

"The stuff or me?"

Shame crossed her features. "Stuff. Everyone thought you died after you didn't come back."

James shrugged. Rodelle visibly relaxed at his reaction. "That's fair. I can live with that. I figured it's better to die after going for a long walk than to rot away in New Eden."

She shifted uncomfortably, digging a toe in the sandy ground, then looked down. "I have something to tell you."

"No shit. I bet you have a lot of stuff to tell me. A lot of time has passed."

"There was an earthquake." Rodelle looked up. "Just over two years ago. Did you feel it here?"

James shook his head. "No."

"It was bad, James. Really bad. Half the remaining population died during the quake. We're down to about twenty people."

James blinked. Brandon held his breath, waiting for his reaction. "Oh. Did Hannah and Jasmine make it?"

"Yes."

"What about Jackson and Lorena?"

Rodelle's answer was uncharacteristically cold. "Jackson didn't. Lorena did."

"I'm sorry to hear that." The easygoing look left James's face, replaced with one of sorrow. A line worried between his brows, and Brandon thought he might actually be telling the truth.

"Have you ever experienced a quake here?" CW44 asked. Brandon was grateful for the change in subject. Judging by the look on Rodelle's face, she was too.

"Nah, not a thing. The south sometimes had little tremors when I lived there, but there hasn't been anything off here, except the storms during the rainy season. They're a lot worse in the north," James replied. "Or maybe I'm just remembering things in the south wrong. It's been a while. So, you came here to look for stuff?"

"I have to back up a bit first. CW44 and Brandon are part of a cybernetic delegation that picked up a distress broadcast Hannah sent out months ago. They were the only people to pick up on it, and . . ."

"Hannah sent out a *broadcast* into space? Holy shit, good for her!"

"It was a miracle. We would have died sooner rather than later if she hadn't. It was *bad* at the settlement." Rodelle looked around the cave again before continuing. "Anyway, the cyborgs had an asteroid home base that was in the path of an ion storm, and they needed somewhere to live off the beaten path. You can't get more off the beaten path than New Eden. We made a deal. They help us rebuild, and in turn, we give them a place to live."

James's gaze settled on Brandon, then on CW44, as if he was truly noticing what they were for the first time. CW44 had ports in his neck that Brandon didn't and still insisted on wearing his black flight suit at all times. He looked like a stereotype of a cyborg in a way that Brandon didn't. "And this is working out?" James finally asked.

"I think so," Rodelle said. "The hydro power station is online, the comms tower is being rebuilt, and we fully expect to have a functioning hospital within the next couple of weeks. CW44 is a medic, in fact."

"There are a couple of us with medical training," the other cyborg replied.

"Jasmine even went out to a deep space waystation for a supply run. She's the first New Edener to leave," Rodelle continued.

The mention of supplies reminded Brandon of why they had taken this journey in the first place. "You said there are other caves with this kind of thing?"

"Yeah, they're all over the place. Jasmine went to space? Not gonna lie, I'm kind of jealous," James said. "Do either of you know what this stuff is for?"

"These are antiquated electrical components," CW44 said. "They could be used for any number of uses."

"Yeah, I thought it was weird that this shit would be here, when the whole point of the settlement was to get away from technology," James said, clearly unimpressed with the things in front of them. "I thought maybe someone else got here earlier, left this stuff behind, and never came back."

"The way the comms tower was destroyed makes us think the settlers didn't intend to cut themselves off from the rest of the universe," Rodelle said. "It's why Hannah was able to teach herself how to rebuild a transmitter without any new supplies." Brandon thought about the SOS the cyborgs had received so many months ago. Hannah had rebuilt a coupler with an old spoon, the only new piece the transmitter required. "We came up here to test out that theory, and since there are boxes of old supplies left behind, we think we were right. Our ancestors weren't afraid of technology and other people. They were probably criminals on the run."

They waited for James's reaction. According to Brandon's internal chronometer, it took seven seconds for him to respond that felt like an eternity. "Huh," was all he managed.

"It's a lot to take in," Rodelle added.

"No shit." James picked up one of the components and turned it over in his hands, as if seeing it in a new light. "Why would they do that?"

"They were probably in legal trouble," Rodelle said, but he cut her off.

"Yeah, I know. I'm speaking figuratively. I just don't get why they would fuck over their families that way. They must have done that, to get them to agree to come here." James tossed away the piece to the ground, where it snapped neatly in half. "I hope that thing isn't too important."

"Even if it was, it's too old to be of any use," CW44 said. The other cyborg's voice was oddly gentle, a rarity for him. "We don't have to talk about this now, if you don't want to. Can you show us the other caves?"

Rodelle and Brandon exchanged a glance, as if to silently ask each other if CW44's brain had been rewired.

"You can look wherever you want," James said.

"Yes, but this is your space. It feels rude to just stomp through the caves. Besides, you know them better than we do." CW44 closed the lid on the box of parts and regarded James curiously. Brandon wondered what he was thinking. Probably wondering how James had kept himself alive as long as he had.

"Yeah, I guess." James thumbed at the cave mouth. "Let me show you the rest of the stuff before it gets dark. You can stay the night in my cave, if you want. It's the only one where the high tide doesn't come in." Without waiting for another word from them, he turned away and led them out of the cave.

The next ones were filled with similar crates, holding other ancient components. Brandon's and CW44's memory banks identified some of them as belonging to older model personal shuttlecraft and shipboard pieces, likely for things like fuel reactors and air recyclers for interstellar travel. They were certainly not the things one would associate with a society determined to be self-sufficient and live off the land.

The last cave they examined was where James had set up his home. The boxes here were much smaller and made of tungsten, a material that Brandon only identified thanks to the cybernetic implants in his palms. James had broken the rubberized seal on one of them, and after Brandon held it, he guessed the only reason James could do that was because it had rotted away due to age. Brandon gingerly opened the lid to reveal a pair of clearscreens. He held them up, surprised they were still intact after so many years.

"You wouldn't happen to know what that is, would you?" James asked. "I thought they might be spaceship windowpanes or something like that, but they're too thin."

"They're portable comp units," CW44 said. He picked up another box and snapped it open with hardly any effort. James looked at him in surprise. CW44 removed another unit from it and held it up. "Very old and very obsolete units."

"What's a comp unit?" James asked.

"Computers," Brandon replied. "Definitely not something I'd expect to see from the kind of people who settled on this planet."

"The age of these corresponds to when the settlers originally came here," CW44 said. "We'll have to take them back with us and see if we can't reactivate them."

James shrugged. "Go ahead. Take whatever you want. Can I come back with you?"

Rodelle looked at him like he'd lost his mind. He had, in a way, if he'd up and wandered off to an unknown wilderness. "Of course you can come back with us. Why the hell wouldn't it be okay?"

Now it was James's turn to look perplexed. "Because I fucked off and let everyone think I was dead? I didn't know if it would be polite to come back."

"I think you'll be pleasantly surprised at how many people will be happy to see you return," Rodelle said. "New Eden is very different now. I mean, it's still in shambles, but the shambles are being repaired and rebuilt. The cyborgs have been very helpful and they're good neighbors." She gave a meaningful glance at Brandon, one that warmed him to his toes. He thought about their kiss in the middle of the night, wondered when and if he would get such an opportunity again.

"We'll take samples of everything when we go back," CW44 said. "We'll start the walk back tomorrow. Does that work for everyone?"

"Whoa," said James. "I'm going home *tomorrow*?"

"Would you rather stay here and make your way back on your own?" CW44 asked.

"Well, no. I should probably go with you. It took me like a week to walk here last time. I'm not sure of the way back."

"What did you see?" Rodelle asked.

James shrugged. "A lot of weird grass and shit."

"What have you been eating all this time?"

"There's a pond farther back with these squishy crab things I've been living off of," James said. "Want some?"

"Crabs?" Rodelle gave him a blank look. "There are *crabs* on New Eden?"

"You've heard of them?"

"I read the same books you did when we were growing up!"

"Oh, yeah. Well, I'm not sure if they're crabs, exactly. They don't really have shells. They live at the bottom of the pond, and they don't make me sick, so . . ." James shrugged. "Breakfast, lunch, and dinner."

A shudder rippled through Brandon. He had long thought the bland, reconstituted excuses that passed for food in the cyborgs' replicators were terrible. Subsisting on weird crab-like bottom feeders for the sole reason that they didn't make him sick sounded like hell.

"Are any of you hungry?" James asked. "It's long past

the time I usually eat supper. I can cook some crabs for you."

Rodelle actually looked intrigued at the notion. "Let us run a scan on the crabs first," Brandon murmured.

"They don't make James sick."

"James has been eating them for the last five years, and his immune system has adapted. Isn't that right, CW44?"

The other cyborg sighed more dramatically than was necessary. Brandon bit back a smile. It was fun to needle him. "Yes and no."

"Tons of crabs to share," James said, as if it was a tempting offer.

"I *am* hungry," Rodelle admitted.

"Then let's eat, *after* we've analyzed the crabs," Brandon said.

As they walked out of the cave behind James, CW44 muttered, "Let's be realistic. After *I've* analyzed the crabs."

FOR THE SECOND night in a row, Rodelle was unable to sleep. She rolled over to see James, who slept in the corner of his cave, wrapped in a blanket he had scavenged from one of the crates when he arrived. He'd learned tonight that it was a heatsaver, often used in utilitarian spaceships that were built without proper crew quarters. It was but one more confirmation that New Eden had been founded by people with something to hide.

There hadn't been any evidence of smuggling yet, which had been one of the original hypotheses after the comms tower was rebuilt. Rodelle was dying to know what was on those clearscreen devices and dearly hoped that any data on them could be retrieved.

How the hell was she expected to sleep after all this?

She rolled over again to her other side, where Brandon lay in his sleep sack on his back. He turned his head to look at her, eyes glowing as his night vision activated. "Hey," he whispered.

"I can't sleep."

"Neither can I."

On the other side of the cave, CW44 released an odd snuffling sound and made a show of turning over in his sleep sack. Rodelle fought the urge to giggle. "Do you think it's safe to go for a walk?"

Brandon's eyes widened, and she wondered what he was thinking. Her breath caught as she waited for his answer. "Sure."

Rodelle didn't need any more encouragement. Both of them shimmied out of their sleep sacks far more quickly than she expected, and on bare feet, walked out of the cave.

Guided by the brightly glowing stars and twin moons overhead, they walked along the beach, the gentle crash of the waves soothing. "Where should we go?" Rodelle asked when they were out of earshot of the cave. Well, James's earshot. He'd lain down and immediately fallen asleep, complete with snoring. CW44 was undoubtedly irritated that he could hear them.

Brandon pointed ahead to the spots James had shown them earlier in the evening. "It's been a long time since I had a shower," Brandon said. "Want to check out one of the hot springs?"

One was the pond filled with the crab creatures, which CW44 announced to be a previously unknown species of freshwater bivalve unique to New Eden, and the other a small hot spring that fed into the ocean. James had mentioned that there were a few such hot springs in the area.

A thrill coursed through Rodelle at the suggestion. "Okay."

Brandon took her hand, threading his fingers through hers, and gently squeezed it. Her breath caught and heart rate increased, which he undoubtedly picked up on. Beneath that, she was a little nervous. She was about to get naked with Brandon. No one had seen her undressed since Jackson.

Don't think about him! She pushed away all thoughts of her dead husband. As if to reassure herself that it was Brandon next to her, that he would never hurt her, she ran her thumb over the back of his hand. He leaned over and lightly nipped her ear in response, sending a jolt of desire through her.

Oh, wow! Her body felt electrified at the small touch, a first for her. Part of her wondered if this was how cyborgs always felt. She clapped her free hand over her mouth to contain her giggle.

"What's so funny?" Brandon asked, his voice low in her ear. Another shiver of pleasure rippled through her.

"I'm just happy, you know?" As Rodelle spoke the words, she realized they were true. She was far from home, seeing a place almost no one else on New Eden had visited, and had rediscovered an old friend while getting closer to new ones. "It's been a long time for me."

In more ways than one. Relatively inexperienced, she hadn't been intimate with anyone except her husband. But judging by the way Brandon slid his arm around her waist, drawing her closer to him, he wouldn't care. He liked her for who she was. Brandon had fought for her, reassured her that he didn't care about her past or that she was a little older than he was. It felt good to be desired.

It also felt good to know this man wouldn't use his body as a weapon against her.

As if he could read her mind, Brandon said, "You don't ever have to do anything you don't want to with me. I like you a lot more than I've liked anyone before. I know you've been through a lot of shit the last couple of years. I don't want to add to it."

His reassurance warmed her in a way she hadn't expected. It oddly fueled her desire for him—a promise that anything that happened would be up to her, that her comfort and safety were paramount. "You wouldn't," she said. "You wouldn't add to the shitshow, I mean. I know you wouldn't do anything that would hurt me." She glanced up at him, mildly surprised to see that his eyes were glowing. Night vision, she supposed. How convenient. The sight of his glowing eyes distracted her for a few seconds, so she didn't notice the pensive look that crossed his face. "Is anything wrong?"

"No, not at all. Believe it or not, I'm actually kind of nervous."

"Why? You're the one who's been trawling through space for the last couple of decades, meeting all kinds of different species."

"Not as much as you'd think."

They walked past the first hot spring they passed, the one that James said he used as his own. Rodelle felt a little weird about invading his space that way, even though he had been amenable to all of them since they'd arrived. They stopped at the second hot spring, about five meters from James's spot. It was larger than James's, lined with a natural rock formation that narrowed toward the ocean. Through the small opening, waves gently crashed against the rocks.

The beach sloped to the spring, the water warm against Rodelle's feet when she took a closer look. Anticipation thrummed through her. With what she hoped was her best coy look, she slipped her oversized tunic over her head and shucked it to the pebbles, far enough away that the spring's gentle waves couldn't touch it. The rest of her clothes followed.

She couldn't believe she had been so brazen.

"Wow," said Brandon, awe in his voice. "You know—I thought about this, and you look better than I could have imagined."

Rodelle had to resist the impulse to giggle. As it was, she walked into the spring, the water's heat and gentle churning a balm to her aching muscles after so many hours of walking.

Brandon was next to strip off his clothes, faster than she would have ever expected. Her breath caught as she took in the sight of him under the light offered by the twin moons. She had seen him shirtless plenty of times—his preferred way of dressing around the settlement—and occasionally let her mind wander about what he looked like without the bottom half of his clothes. Metal pieces embedded in his skin glinted in the moonlight, another reminder of what he was. The muscles in his powerfully built thighs flexed as he walked toward her, an assurance in his step. She forced herself not to look between them, not wanting to be rude. Yet.

Brandon glided into the water after her, surprise blooming on his face as the water's temperature registered. Just as quickly, he recovered, his expression replaced by blatant need.

Rodelle held her breath, anticipation racing through her veins. She didn't release it until he touched her, his hand reaching for her ear to tuck an errant strand of hair behind it. Sparks skittered down her skin, so powerful that, if she didn't know any better, she would have thought he had activated the tech in his hands.

His arm slid around her waist to bring her closer to him, his free hand tilting her chin. His mouth slanted over hers, kissing her with an intensity and confidence that drew a mewl from her throat. Her knees went weak. If Brandon hadn't been holding on to her, she might have slid into the water.

Rodelle quickly recovered, regaining her footing before she could slip away. The water wasn't deep, only reaching her waist, but the last thing she wanted was to fall face down in it again. She put everything she could into her response, tongue demanding entrance to his mouth, which he was only too happy to offer. Her nipples stiffened, scraping against his broad chest, the sensation drawing a gasp of pleasure against his lips. Brandon responded, body rearing into her, his substantial erection pressing into her belly.

Anticipation rippled through her, and with it, a curious boldness. She broke their kiss so she could look at him, his eyes still luminous in the light overhead. Drawing a finger down his chest, she marveled at the smooth planes of his skin. He sucked in a harsh breath, a smile playing across his lips as she explored his body, dipping her hand lower to lightly graze her fingertips down his waist, across his hipbones, to his erection that still pressed against her. After hesitating for half a second, she wrapped her hand around it, lightly gliding along his shaft.

Brandon's response was immediate. A strangled sound escaped from him as he thrust into her hand, and he reached for her shoulder to steady himself. "Sorry," he said through gritted teeth. A wolfish smile bloomed on his face, an expression that hinted that there could be so much more between them. "I've imagined you doing that for a while now."

A thrill coursed through Rodelle at that admission. She

felt a little heady to know she could wield that power over him. "You have?" Encouraged, she slid her hand along his cock again, a motion that teased another heated look from him.

"I think, by now, you know damn well that I have," Brandon replied, voice strained. "If you keep that up, this is going to be over soon. Not that I'm complaining, but if you want anything else to happen tonight . . ."

A tiny spark of nervousness flared in Rodelle at the implication. "I'm not sure I'm ready for that yet."

"That's fine. I meant it when I said we'll take things at your speed."

Rodelle tightened her grip just a little as she stroked him. "Can we keep doing this? I just—I want to explore you."

"Are you fucking kidding me right now?" She bit back a smile. "Of course, you can do this whenever you want." He covered her hand with his, guiding her. "Like that. Oh, God!"

Rodelle didn't stop. He didn't let go of her as his body shook, nearly vibrating against her. He pressed his lips to hers as he stiffened with his release. Leaning against her, he pressed a kiss to her neck, one hand buried in her braid. His heart beat a rapid tattoo against her, his skin hot. "That was unexpected," he said when he caught his breath. "Thank you."

"That was fun," she agreed.

"More for me than you. I'm feeling pretty guilty right now, to be honest with you." He straightened, then pulled her to him in a hug.

"Why?"

"Because I'd thought about this night going a little differently. Something more for your pleasure, you know?"

"I enjoyed that," she said. "I like making you come undone."

"Is that what we're calling it? I'd planned to do that to you. Can I get a rain check sometime?"

"What's a rain check?"

He chuckled, the sound vibrating through her. "I don't know. I think it's something my original used to say. I think it's asking to get something later?"

"Yes." A new wave of excitement swelled in her at the notion. "I want that, very much."

CHAPTER SEVEN

James tugged at the black flight trousers that sagged around his hips and legs. They were CW44's spare pair, clothes James had reluctantly donned at Rodelle's urging. Just because he was used to being naked all the time didn't mean that the rest of the settlement would be too. Seeing their old friend alive was enough of a surprise without throwing nudity into the mix. "Are you sure I have to wear these?" he grumbled to Rodelle. He'd muttered a variation of that complaint since they set off for home nearly two days ago.

"Yes." She adjusted her pack's straps, looking forward to finally being able to toss it away for good. At least the load was lighter. James had a small bag on his back, filled with the clearscreens from the caves and some of her supplies. He'd offered to take them over her protests, then got into an argument with CW44 about bringing back some of the crabs. Apparently, they wouldn't be safe to eat, although James insisted that his constitution was hardy enough to handle old meat.

Brandon and CW44 had walked ahead of them for

most of the trip, and Rodelle missed chatting with Brandon. Heat suffused her whenever she thought about their too-brief interlude away from the caves, and with it, a desperate need to pick up where they left off. She knew why he was keeping his distance—he was giving her space with James, an opportunity to fill him in on what had happened to the settlement in his absence.

Unfortunately, James wasn't one for listening. Over the last two days of walking, he'd changed the subject whenever Rodelle tried to tell him about the earthquake or how things had changed, instead preferring to tell her about what he'd been up to the last few years. Which wasn't much, other than meditating, sleeping, singing, perfecting his cartwheel skills on the beach, and eating questionable seafood. Other than his sunburn and looking too thin—which most New Edeners did—he seemed otherwise healthy.

"You said the settlement is different," James groused. "Maybe they won't mind that I'm not used to wearing clothes anymore."

"You have to wear clothes for now." Rodelle struggled to keep the exasperation out of her voice. The back and forth brought to mind the times when they were younger, when she was the babysitter roped into looking after him, Hannah, and Jasmine. James was always the one she'd had to keep a close eye on. He'd had a tendency to wander off to the protests of everyone.

Thinking back to their youth reminded her of Hannah, and how she and James had once had a history together, as much as they'd tried and failed to hide their relationship. "There's something I have to tell you about Hannah," she said, voice low and urgent.

James halted in his tracks. Big blue eyes looked at her beseechingly. "Oh, my God, was she hurt?"

"No."

"She's okay, right?"

"Yes."

"She isn't mad at me for going to the north?"

"Doubtful, since she had no idea you were alive. She was sad when you disappeared. We all were."

His brow furrowed. "Didn't you get my note?"

"The one written on the wall in the community center? Yes, but that's not my point. Hannah's in a pretty serious relationship with one of the cyborg, Rhys. He's their leader."

James's brows lifted so high, they touched his over-grown hair. "Oh, damn. Good for her. You know we split up way before I went on my walk, right? I'm happy she's moved on."

"I hope your return won't send her into a heart attack. We don't have the resources to treat that yet."

Ahead of them, CW44 called over his shoulder, "Give me some credit. I can handle treating a myocardial infarction."

"You're a doctor?" James asked. Holding his trousers up against his hips, he ran ahead to catch up with CW44 and Brandon, his bare feet slapping against the ground. Rodelle cringed. That had to hurt. Or maybe not. The soles of his feet had to be tougher than the reused leather scraps they made their sandals out of at the settlement.

CW44's response was even, clipped. "I'm a medic."

"Can you scan me for diseases? I have this eye thing that's been bugging me for a couple years now."

The set of the cyborg's shoulders stiffened for a second. "I'll see what I can do for you in our ship's sickbay."

"Oh, yeah, I guess that means you have a spaceship too. That's awesome! Can I see it?" His trousers sagged again, and James yanked them up. "Sorry. It really would be easier for me if I could just forget the pants, yeah?"

"For God's sake," muttered Rodelle. She picked up her pace to catch up with the others, striding alongside Brandon. He looked like he was trying not to laugh. "You know what? We're not supposed to arrive until tomorrow morning, anyway. James, you may as well take off your pants if it means you can keep up without complaining."

"Awesome." Without another word, James halted and threw his pack to the ground with a carelessness that made CW44 cringe. He stripped off his trousers and tied the legs around his waist. "Much better."

"I can civilize you when we get back," Rodelle promised.

"Nah, you can't. It's not nice to lie. You taught me that, remember?"

She didn't remember, but she nodded, anyway. It sounded like something she would've said as a teenage babysitter.

Rodelle glanced at James. He was trying to keep up with CW44. A few centimeters shorter than the cyborg, he couldn't quite keep up with CW44's strides. "Can you check my eye now?" James asked. There was a note of worry in his voice for the first time since their meeting on the beach.

"Is it bothering you now?" Rodelle asked.

"Yeah, like I'm worried that I might be sick," James replied.

A muscle ticked in CW44's jaw. "I cannot conduct an examination under these circumstances."

"I didn't expect so, but could you tell me if I'm dying or something? I didn't stress about it before, because I figured I'd break my leg again and die of an infection or something, like everyone else at the settlement. But now that there's a possibility I might not die of something stupid, I'm kind of concerned, you know?"

Brandon sighed. "You have a handheld in your pack, don't you?"

"Of course. I would never leave the ship without one." CW44 sounded appalled at the prospect.

Rodelle didn't know what "handheld" referred to, but hopefully, it was an instrument that could tell if James was sick. "Maybe you need glasses," she suggested.

"I bet half the planet needed glasses. That doesn't mean we'd have the means to get them," James said.

"What the hell are glasses?" Brandon asked.

"Lenses in a frame that are worn over your eyes to correct vision," Rodelle explained. "The frame goes over the bridge of your nose."

"Yeah, I'm still not sure what you're talking about." Brandon sounded confused. "Do you have them here?"

"Maybe an old antique pair lying around in an abandoned house. I've mostly seen them in pictures and books," Rodelle said. "I'll draw you a picture sometime."

"No, I don't think this is because I need glasses, although I'm pretty sure I could use a pair. I get weird spots in my left one sometimes," James said. "Like someone's dropped a blob of black paint in my eye."

Brandon nudged CW44 in the side. "Come on. Help him out."

CW44 looked at James, disdain written across his features. Nude save for the black trousers tied around his waist and pack strapped to his back, he looked ridiculous. Or would have, had he not gone pale under his sunburn. Tension lines bracketed his mouth.

CW44 paused and closed his eyes for a few seconds. Brandon's eyes hadn't taken on an unsettling silvery hue, which meant they weren't speaking to each other telepathically. When CW44's opened, they were still their usual hazel. "We have to make camp soon. Once we have done that, I will see to your eye with the limited resources I have."

James's shoulders sagged with relief. "Thanks, man. Appreciate it."

"We have another five kilometers to walk before we can do so. There's a river close to where we'll set up."

"Is that the river we crossed on the way to the caves?" Rodelle asked.

CW44 nodded.

"I promise I won't fall on my face again."

"I promised to carry you across it," Brandon reminded her. An unexpected bolt of heat coursed through Rodelle as she remembered his strength, so effortless.

"Five kilometers," CW44 barked. "Let's go. Perhaps it will be easier if each of us picks up one of you and we run."

"We're running a little low on rations," Brandon pointed out. "I don't know about you, but I'm feeling effects of physical exertions and the lack of decent food."

"I bet," muttered CW44.

"I was referring to all the walking and running," Brandon quickly explained. But the heated look he sent in Rodelle's direction said otherwise. "If we keep going at this pace, I'll be fine until we get back to the settlement. If we speed things up, I'm going to have to shift over to auxiliary power, and it'll take forever for me to get back to normal."

"Whoa," said James, wide-eyed. "How does that work?"

"Brandon can explain it as we walk," CW44 said, voice curt. He pointed ahead, between a pair of gnarled blue-leaved trees. "Onward."

———

BRANDON LAY ON HIS BACK, gaze trained on the stars above as he felt himself drift off to sleep. A meter away, Rodelle was curled on her side under her sleep sack. Her breathing was deep and even in slumber, a sign that she trusted him. Brandon's heart swelled, and with it, a bolt of desire shot through him as he remembered their interlude in the hot spring. They hadn't had any time alone together since then.

James was a few meters away, his snoring carrying over their campsite. CW44 had conducted a perfunctory exam when they set up their camp but didn't make a diagnosis. Brandon had recognized the way the other cyborg's lips had thinned when he declined to answer James's questions, promising to make one after he'd had a chance to examine James more thoroughly when they returned to the settlement. If Rodelle or James had noticed CW44's caginess, they hadn't let on. But it was pulling at Brandon.

He tested out their shared link. *Are you awake?*

A few seconds later, CW44 replied. *I was meditating in an attempt to sleep, but I suppose I can talk. Is this about James's eye?*

Yes.

Another pause. *Do not speak of this to him or Rodelle yet, but I'm fairly certain he has some type of ocular malignancy.*

A chill slithered down Brandon's spine.

Eye cancer, CW44 added.

I know. Holy fuck, that's awful. Is he terminal?

Probably not, but I'd have to do more tests to find out.

How would he develop such a disease?

Brandon thought he could hear CW44's shrug. *Genetic susceptibility, ultraviolet radiation exposure from the suns, environmental factors in the north. There are a few causes of it. I don't know of any other humanoid cultures that haven't developed vaccines for cancers or eradicated them altogether through genetic therapies. New Eden is novel.*

How would it be treated?

I don't know yet. Surgery is in my purview, although I would have to do more research into how to treat eye cancer. Of course, I wouldn't want to leave him blind or maimed.

Don't you have any data on it saved?

No. I'm not Darius. I don't keep my head clogged with endless files of books and cartoons. I'll have to wait until I get back to the ship and see if I can't look up eye cancer treatments there.

Could you take him off-world to a waystation with a hospital? Brandon pressed.

Yes, although I don't know what medical facility in the galaxy would know how to treat it. CW44 was silent for a few seconds, probably sighing to himself. *He has options on New Eden.*

A cloned eyeball?

It's a little more nuanced than that, but a cloned eye is a possibility. There was another pause. *Would it bother you if I resume my meditating? I prefer to commune with the stars before I sleep.*

Despite the unexpected gravity of the situation, Brandon couldn't keep a smile from his face. CW44 was the only person he had ever met who was remotely spiritual. His original, whoever he was, had probably been quite the religious man if CW44 still felt the need to pray to stars. *You do you.*

Thank you for your approval. Good night, Brandon.

Brandon turned over to better face Rodelle. Something in him warmed at the sight, how peaceful she looked in sleep. He wiggled a little closer to her, shifting his sleep sack with his body. She stirred, then blinked. Lifting her head, she murmured an unintelligible, "Mm-hmm?"

A few meters away, James continued snoring, heedless of the probable disease he had.

"Everything's all right," Brandon whispered. "Go back to sleep."

She turned half-lidded eyes to him. Her voice was a whisper, rough from sleep. "Okay." Leaning closer, she asked, "Can you kiss me good night?"

CW44's voice popped into Brandon's head. *For the love of God!*

Tell that to the stars, Brandon quickly replied. He hoped Rodelle didn't notice his eyes changing as he did so. To his relief, she angled herself closer to him instead. "Of course. You don't have to ask," he murmured aloud before pressing his lips to hers.

The feel of her was electric. Though the kiss was almost chaste, it reminded Brandon of everything they had shared at the caves, of what he was looking forward to when they returned home. Rodelle Lansing was a delight, a gift, one he could hardly wait to unwrap.

He reluctantly broke away. She turned a sleepy smile on him before laying her head down and drawing her sleep sack around her. Brandon stayed on his side, watching her until he felt himself nod off.

CHAPTER EIGHT

THE LONG, blue-green grass gently swayed in the breeze, a welcome sight that meant they were closer to home. Excitement thrummed through Rodelle as the native foliage gave way to the familiar green grass of the settlement, overgrown in this part of it. The restored comms tower came into view, its blue glass window shining in the sunlight. The launch pad had been rebuilt in their absence, too, and a black spaceship rested on it. Rodelle halted and blinked, hardly able to believe her eyes. It was smaller than the one the cyborgs had arrived on, more angular. Like the original ship design had been improved on. "Is that yours?" she asked, pointing.

Brandon, CW44, and James also stopped to gawk. "No," Brandon replied. His voice was wary.

Rodelle's excitement gave way to fear. "What do you think it is?"

Brandon's lips thinned. "I wish I could tell you."

"That isn't your ship?" James asked.

"No," CW44 replied. "It's very similar to ours, though. Perhaps they were built at the same shipyard."

"Can't you scan it or whatever?" James asked. He had been very curious about CW44's medical equipment, scant as it was. The memory of James's fascination and CW44's cagey answers afterward pulled at her. She had the sneaking suspicion that the cyborg knew more about James's condition than he was letting on.

"Not from this distance with the equipment I have," CW44 replied, voice tight. "I feel really stupid now that we didn't think to take weapons with us on the trip."

"New Eden doesn't have any predators," Brandon pointed out. "Or native animals that can be killed for food, aside from those crabs."

"I really wish I could've brought some back with us," muttered James.

Well, there had been one predator, Rodelle thought. But Jackson was dead now, thanks to her. Anxiety over the memory mingled with her fear of what was in the settlement. Aside from her brief exchange with Brandon at the river, she'd managed to go days without thinking of her husband, for the first time since the earthquake.

"Could it be other cyborgs?" she asked. "Maybe there are other clones you don't know of."

Brandon and CW44 were quiet for a few seconds. A glance at them told Rodelle they weren't speaking telepathically. "Well, fuck," Brandon said. "I never thought of that."

"Look, nothing is on fire and no one is screaming," Rodelle said. "Maybe this is a friendly designation or there's a mix-up or something. I think we should just go there, see what's happening, and figure out what to do from there."

"Maybe we should go to our ship for weaponry," CW44 suggested.

"Negative to that. We'd have to pass the ship at the

comms tower to get to ours. If it's here for the wrong reasons, we would be seen, anyway." Brandon scrubbed a hand over his face. "Look, I hate to say it, but I think the best way to approach this is to get close enough to the settlement that we can speak to another cyborg over our link and find out what's going on."

James looked uneasy for the first time since they'd found him. CW44's jaw was clenched and Brandon's expression was unreadable. A strange sense of responsibility came over Rodelle. She'd been living in the settlement the longest, had seen it destroyed. The fleeting thought that this must be how Hannah felt toward their home crossed her mind.

"Maybe it isn't all bad," she said. "Let's go. As soon as you two get in range, tell us what the others are saying." She started walking again, only to have Brandon grab her arm. The look in his eyes was almost feral, but instead of feeling panicked and cornered, she felt safe. Like he was a man determined to protect her at all costs.

Without a word, he kissed her fiercely. Before she could react, he let go of her. For half a second, she thought her knees would give way beneath her. She took a deep breath, then a step forward, relieved that her legs were still working. A curious combination of desire and bravery filled her, a determination that both of them would live through this, to give in to what she had been daydreaming about since she met him. The stormy expression on Brandon's face told her he was thinking the same thing.

Side by side, they walked toward the settlement, CW44 and James trailing behind them. The cyborgs' starship was in its usual spot, its ramp extended from its airlock and cargo bays yawing open. Cautious optimism filled Rodelle. The settlement wasn't on fire, nor were there bodies strewn around. "Maybe everything's okay," she said aloud. Brandon reached for her hand and quickly squeezed it.

Before he could try to speak to the other cyborgs via their link, the barn door opened. New Eden's residents spilled out in all directions. Relief poured through Rodelle when she saw Hannah and Jasmine among them. She bolted in their direction. "Hey!"

Jasmine's face was flushed with excitement. "Did you see the Si'laar?" she asked by way of greeting.

"No. Is that the other ship in the field?" Rodelle was so relieved to see that her friends and home were all right that she couldn't keep herself from babbling. "There's so much I have to tell you!"

Jasmine and Hannah exchanged a look. "Did you find answers in the north?"

"Oh, my God. You have no idea." Rodelle glanced behind her. Brandon, CW44, and James lingered a few meters away. James fiddled with his trousers waistband, his red hair shining in the sunlight.

Beneath her tan, Hannah paled. "Is that . . ."

Jasmine let out a strangled noise Rodelle couldn't identify. "What the fuck?"

"There's more," Rodelle said. "We found some equipment in the caves that anti-tech zealots definitely wouldn't have had use for, and . . ." Her words died in her throat when a tall, slender figure wearing a long, hooded robe stepped out of the barn. "Sorry, you said something about the—is that the Si'laar you were talking about? What's a Si'laar?"

Simon emerged from the barn and reached for Jasmine's hand. "The people our previous iterations stole their ship from."

"What?" Rodelle glanced at the figure again. Two

more had joined it. "Okay. Wow. A lot has happened in the last few days."

"Yeah, no shit." Without another word, Hannah strode to James, who flinched when he saw her. Half a second later, his face broke out in a grin, and he threw his skinny arms around her. Hannah visibly stiffened for a moment before she hugged him back.

Jasmine dashed to where they stood, eagerly wrapping James in a hug of her own. Rodelle looked around at the New Edeners who alternated gaping at James and the giant robed aliens in turn, as if they had no idea where to look. Neither did Rodelle.

"Should we introduce ourselves?" Brandon murmured in Rodelle's ear. She jumped, unaware that he was behind her.

"Excuse our lack of manners." Rhys appeared in the crowd. "Korjek is the leader of the Si'laar designation. Come with me."

"Did we steal their ship?" Brandon asked as he followed, Rodelle close behind.

"Sort of." Without offering further explanation, Rhys stopped in front of one of the aliens. "Their physiology cannot tolerate New Eden's daytime conditions for extended periods, so this will have to be brief. Korjek, this is Brandon Emerson, formerly BE89, and Rodelle Lansing, the widow of New Eden's late leader."

Something twisted in Rodelle's gut at the mention of Jackson. She pasted what she hoped was a friendly smile on her face and nodded at them in greeting. "It's a pleasure to meet you."

"I feel like I should apologize for the ship," Brandon muttered.

An odd clicking noise sounded from under Korjek's hood. "Our greetings to you, likewise." Their voice was quiet and raspy, almost a hiss, a strange crackling under-current beneath it. "There is much to discuss about our stolen technology, but it will have to wait until a later time when we can be earthbound."

Earthbound? Rodelle sneaked a glance at Brandon, who looked as mystified as she felt. Did they fly?

"There is no need for worry," Korjek added. "We are here for the same reason as your people and have arrived peacefully. We will return to our ship for now. After the suns have set, we can safely emerge again, and we will see about establishing a colony in your western sea."

Rhys nodded, like he understood what the alien was saying. They lived in *water?*

"If you need help, let me know. I don't mind deep water," Brandon offered. Rhys faintly shuddered.

The alien shuffled away, joining the rest of their small delegation. A couple of cyborgs accompanied them, as well as Ollie West, oddly enough, who actually seemed delighted at New Eden's latest inhabitants. Weird.

To Rhys, Brandon said, "We found out a great deal on the trip to the north."

Rhys raised an eyebrow. "And an unaccounted-for New Edener."

"Yeah, he's sort of messed up," said Rodelle. "Like, in a different way than the rest of us are."

A shadow crossed Brandon's face at the mention of James, and she wondered again what he wasn't telling her.

"We brought back clearscreens we found in the caves," Brandon continued.

"That's hardly the kind of tech I would expect to see from New Eden settlers," Rhys replied.

"No, it isn't. They're inoperable, of course, but there must be a way to retrieve their data on our ship."

"I would expect so, since the original New Eden settlers

had business with some of our previous iterations." Rhys's voice was impassive, neutral, like he hadn't just dropped another bombshell on them.

It took a few seconds for his words to make their impact. "What?" yelped Rodelle.

"We discovered evidence of previous collusion when the comms tower was brought back online," Rhys explained.

"Okay, but that's still a hell of a thing to tell us!"

"Jasmine took the news very well," Rhys said, confused. "So did Hannah."

Chastised, Rodelle sighed. "I'm sorry. I didn't mean to blow up at you. I'm not Jasmine or Hannah, and I don't think I'm taking it badly. Between that, the Si'laar, James, and all the weird shit we found hidden in the caves, I'm just at my capacity for surprises, you know?"

Rhys nodded, unperturbed. "Understood. Brandon, please take the clearscreens back to our ship. We can extract their data there. What else was in the north?"

Brandon gave a pointed look over his shoulder, where James was talking the ear off of Ollie, who had stopped trailing the Si'laar to say hello. Wonder of wonders, he was listening and nodding with rapt attention. CW44 stood to the side, looking bewildered at their exchange. Rodelle couldn't help but smile a little. Ollie and James were distantly related, she recalled. Maybe third cousins? She wasn't sure.

Catching her glance, CW44 approached them. "I hear you're going back to the ship. I should bring James back to the ship as well," he said quietly. There was a grave note to his voice, cementing Rodelle's suspicion that James was sick.

"We're on our way there now," Brandon said.

"Can I go?" she asked.

Brandon looked at her as if she was nuts. "Of course."

"I haven't had a chance to really look at the ship," she said, hoping he didn't notice the waver in her voice, a sure sign she was nervous. "Plus, I want to see what's on those clearscreen things."

"It could take a while for us to figure out how to activate them," Brandon warned her. "Don't you want to head back to the house first, maybe get something to eat?"

Her shoulders ached at the reminder of the pack strapped to her back. She'd forgotten all about it. "Yeah. Let's unload everything at the ship first, though."

Brandon nodded. "It's up to you. Let's go."

She walked alongside him through the settlement to the field where their ship waited. A few people, cyborgs and New Edeners together, were carrying out cartons and directing anti-grav pallets loaded with stuff. The faint lowing of cattle faintly sounded from the open cargo bays, a noise Rodelle hadn't heard since before the quake. "They brought *cows* back?" she asked in astonishment.

Behind her, James chortled. "Huh. Cows."

Rodelle didn't question why he found the notion funny. He'd been wandering around the wilderness for years, after all.

"I miss my crabs," James added.

"Your diet will improve now that you're back home," CW44 said briskly. They walked up the exterior ramp and through the open airlock. Rodelle blinked at the abrupt change in light, her vision taking a few seconds to adjust.

Their footsteps echoed off the metal deck that snaked through the ship. As they turned down a corridor, CW44 abruptly said, "We'll be going to the sickbay now." He pressed a panel in the wall with his fingertip. It slid open with a near-silent hiss, revealing a landing with a short staircase. To James, he said, "Follow me."

James nodded, his red curls bobbing. A grin split his face. "Thank you. I hope this won't hurt."

CW44 made a noncommittal noise and descended the stairs. James waved at Rodelle and Brandon before following.

The panel hissed closed. Rodelle peered at the wall, noticing the faint seams that marked the door, barely visible to the naked eye. "Wow," she murmured.

"There are other ways to get to the other decks, but this is the fastest from the airlock. We have lifts," Brandon explained.

They resumed walking again. "Brandon?" she whispered.

He paused and faced her, uncertainty across his face. "Yes?"

"Is something wrong with James?"

Brandon looked away for a few seconds, long enough for Rodelle to know that her suspicions were correct. Her stomach dropped. "Oh, my God," she said softly. "Is he dying?"

"No!" Brandon's response was vehement, probably louder than he intended. His next words were quieter. "CW44 has reason to believe he needs medical attention. I know everyone on New Eden does, but James may have some unique health concerns that need to be checked out by a medic. He did tell all of us that he had dark spots in one of his eyes."

"What could be wrong with him?" she pressed.

"There are a few things," Brandon said, not meeting her gaze.

"Brandon." She put her hand on her hip, trying to look as authoritative as she could.

He glanced up and down the corridor, as if he was worried about being overheard. "Come with me."

He led her through the corridor to a large room dominated by consoles, their lights lazily blinking an array of colors. "Give me your pack," Brandon commanded.

She did so, realizing that, once again, she had forgotten that the damn thing was strapped to her back. "What do you think is wrong with James?"

Brandon had shucked off his own and unsealed it, pulling out clearscreens and other gadgets from the caves that Rodelle couldn't identify. He opened hers and did the same with the tech stashed there. "CW44 asked me to keep this to myself," he began. "But I can't lie to you. I'm telling you this with the assumption you're not going to repeat anything."

Her heart thudded against her ribs. "Of course."

"James's symptoms are consistent with an ocular growth. Possibly a malignancy. Do you know what that is?"

A wave of nausea crested over Rodelle as the impact of his words sank in. Tears sprang to her eyes, and she had to speak around a lump that formed in her throat. "I know what cancer is. I think some people here might have died from it."

"James isn't dying," Brandon said. "He needs medical attention, and that's CW44's forte, as well as a few other cyborgs. He's in as good hands as he can get right now."

"What if he can't be treated?"

"That's a big if, and *if* that's the case, I'm sure we'll arrange to take him to a hospital at a waystation. Look, Rodelle, I promised CW44 I wouldn't say anything about James's condition. You need to keep this to yourself and keep it together."

She nodded and impatiently brushed away tears with the back of her hand. "I promise." She tried to smile. "If you say he'll be okay, I'll believe you."

Something in Brandon's expression relaxed. "Come here." He held out his arms.

Rodelle was only too happy to let him hold her. He pressed a kiss to the top of her head. "I know this is hard, finding your friend after so long, then finding out that he's sick."

"I used to babysit him," she said into his chest. She took a deep breath, his scent unmistakable under the woodsy smell he now had after traipsing around the wilderness for days.

"I need a bath," Brandon said, as if he'd guessed what she'd just done. "You don't smell too bad, though. And what do you mean by babysitting?"

"Child minding, I guess. I was the oldest girl in our generation, so I got to look after Hannah, Jasmine, and James when we were younger. There were a few other kids along the way, but . . ." Her voice trailed off, and with it, a corresponding pain gripped her heart as she thought of them, gone far too young, lost to accidents and fevers.

Brandon was quiet for a moment, digesting this. "And you had to do that because you were the girl?"

The question surprised her. The old indignant feeling that she locked away whenever someone's parent ordered her to look after their child sprang up, long forgotten until now. "Yes."

"The man who eventually became your husband—he didn't help?"

"No."

"Because he was a boy?"

She nodded against his chest. "Yeah."

"That's fucked up."

A harsh, mirthless laugh escaped her. "What part of this planet isn't?"

"Good point." His arms tightened around her. "Look,

CW44 said James isn't dying, and whatever he has is likely treatable with what we have in the sickbay. I know you're worried, but remember that he's in good hands. CW44 knows what he's doing."

Rodelle took a watery breath and tried to compose herself. "I know." She reluctantly pulled away to look at the pile of tech around them. "What happens now?"

"CW44 conducts an exam on James's eye, and I connect the clearscreens to our comp banks and dump all the data in them into our ship. And after *that*, I think it's time to go home and get some rest."

An odd flutter raced through her at the thought of going home with him. How were things going to change after everything that had happened? Rodelle felt the heat of desire rise in her, a need for him that she had never had for anyone else. The memory of their time in the hot spring sprang to mind, and with it, a dozen secret fantasies that she'd never told a soul, could never *dream* of telling a soul. Except Brandon.

"Okay." Her voice came out in a breathy whisper. "When can we go?"

CHAPTER NINE

The ramshackle Lansing house was exactly as Brandon remembered it—the remaining wooden shingle siding falling apart, its ancient yellow paint peeling; the front window boarded up; random sprouts of patchy grass that he now knew wasn't native to New Eden. But this time, returning to it with Rodelle, the old place sort of felt like home. Opening the front door, he was greeted by the faint odor of the doughnuts they had baked together before leaving for the north.

And, he noticed with satisfaction, Rodelle followed him right into the house, instead of making a beeline for the shed that she had been sleeping in for as long as he'd known her.

"Are you hungry?" he asked, shucking off his pack.

"Hungry, dirty, and tired," she replied. "Do you want to take a bath first, or should I?"

"We could go together." He tried to put as much suggestion into his voice as he could. His senses picked up her minute gasp, then she bit her lip in a way that made him want to kiss her. More than he usually did, anyway.

"I—" She looked away for a moment, and he wondered what he had said wrong.

"We don't have to," he quickly added. His heartbeat picked up speed. Dimly, he was aware of his cybernetics reminding him that the cause for it was unknown. *Stupid computer*, he thought. Unable to distinguish between physical aberrations and aberrations caused by emotional reactions.

"It's not that," Rodelle said. "Can I take a rain check?"

He smiled, remembering their earlier banter at the hot spring. "Of course." He hesitated, choosing his next words carefully. "I like you a lot. I always have. I know you've had a rough go of it for years."

"Forever," she said wryly.

"Right. Whenever you're ready—*if* you're ready—I'll be waiting." He held his breath. Another warning from his cybernetics faintly clanged, reminding him to breathe. He ignored it.

"I know." She stood up on tiptoes to press a kiss to his cheek. "I just need some time to think about what we've seen over the last few days. It's a lot."

"I get it." Brandon wondered how James was doing, how CW44 had delivered his probable cancer diagnosis. "Your friend will be fine."

"Physically, maybe. He's spent the last five years doing nude cartwheels in the sand. I'm not sure his mind is all there." She shook her head a little. "Don't mind me. I'm taking a bath. I won't be too long."

"Take all the time you want. I'm going to see about making something for a snack. I don't know about you, but I will happily go to my grave before surviving on cubes again."

"Brandon, it wasn't even a week eating them."

"Any meal of nutritionally balanced freeze dried foodstuffs is one too many. Go take your bath," he urged. "When you get out, I'll have something for us."

She smiled. "Thank you."

Rodelle turned and left the kitchen, disappearing through the short corridor that led to the main bedroom and bathroom. A few seconds later, the pipes groaned as she started running water into the tub. There were a couple of smaller rooms off the corridor that Brandon supposed could have been used as bedrooms, albeit tiny ones. They were empty, save for old bric-a-brac that he guessed had belonged to Rodelle's late husband's family once upon a time.

Brandon washed his hands at the sink, a fixture that still used a water pump. Then he took stock of the supplies in the pantry and icebox—eggs from New Eden hens, sugar berries native to the planet, a can of flour he'd filched from the cyborgs' ship's last supply run to the nearest waystation. Some powdered milk from cloned cows, tomatoes and peppers from the planet's agri-center, grown and harvested by Hannah, some naroki strips he'd preserved in cooking oil after he'd roasted the meat in Rodelle's yard for breakfast. It felt like such a long time ago.

Baking something would take too much time. Rodelle's old oven took far too long to reach the right temperature. Instead, Brandon hauled out a heavy iron pan, old and well-seasoned, likely a family relic since before they'd landed on New Eden. He'd never seen evidence of an iron-works or a way to mine iron ore.

His original had loved vintage iron cooking imple-ments, he recalled. Brayden Emerson had loved all things gastronomic. Brandon occasionally had old memories resurface of a collection of cast iron and copper pans and pots, lovingly used and cared for.

After winding the temperature gauge on the stovetop, he set the pan on its single burner and waited for it to heat. He assembled the ingredients for an omelet, dicing a pepper that looked a little wrinkly and chopping a couple of tomatoes. He cracked a few eggs in a bowl—ceramic, he noted with appreciation—adding some reconstituted powdered milk, then stirred it with a fork. Pouring the mixture into the hot pan, he added the vegetables and naroki strips. It was a shame he didn't have any cheese.

While the eggs quietly bubbled in the pan, he boiled some water and made a cup of tea. *That's one cube I don't mind*, he thought as he inhaled the familiar aroma. He poked through the drawers underneath the scarred kitchen counter, looking for a spatula and coming up empty. He'd have to remember to create one in the ship's replicator.

He improvised with a pair of flat knives, one in each hand, flipping half the omelet over itself before taking the pan off the stove. The burner still glowed red, slowly fading as its power wound down. Taking a seat at the table, he sipped his tea and waited for Rodelle. Desire thrummed through him as he thought about her in the tub, water sluicing over her skin . . .

A gurgle sounded through the house as water flowed through the old pipes, a sign that Rodelle had drained the tub. A few moments later, she appeared in the kitchen doorway. She was barefoot, her long blonde hair still damp and loose, wearing a thin tunic that Brandon recognized as one of Jasmine's recent creations. "Something smells good," she said.

"I made an omelet for us to share. Help yourself."

She shook her head. "I can wait for you. Go take a bath."

"Do I really smell that bad?"

She gave him a withering look. "You know you don't. I just want to have a meal with you."

He rose and drained the last of his tea. "You're adorable." Color touched her cheeks, and she smiled shyly. "There are cubes and plenty of hot water left in the kettle, if you want some coffee or tea." He traced the back of his hand along her cheek, relishing the faint shudder of pleasure that rippled through her. Closing her eyes, she leaned into him. "I won't be long."

———

RODELLE'S NERVOUSNESS had mostly washed away with her bathwater down the drain, replaced by excitement and a curiosity she'd never felt with anyone else. She'd been discomfited when they returned home, the reminders of Jackson still in the house—the housewares that had belonged to his family, the home itself that had been built by his many times over great grandparents. The house that Jackson's sister Lorena hadn't wanted when he died. A house that Rodelle hadn't wanted, either.

That old sense of guilt pulled at her again, a reminder of her role in Jackson's death, the secret she would carry to her grave. She took a deep swallow of tea, willing it away. She had spent years in bed overrun with shame, even though, in retrospect, Jackson had deserved it. If he had survived the quake, he would have eventually killed her, she was sure of it. His abuse had worsened in the months leading to the quake, getting more physical as he escalated from occasional slaps to his using his fists. He'd started leaving marks on her.

The familiar gurgle of the house's antiquated plumbing told her Brandon had finished his bath as quickly as he'd promised he would be. Rodelle pushed away all thoughts of Jackson, focusing on the meal ahead of them, and hopefully, something more. A frisson of lust had goose bumps popping up along her skin, a thrill of anticipation she'd never experienced before.

A few moments later, he returned to the kitchen, wearing a clean pair of the black flight trousers he always favored. The metal components in his chest and arms shone dully in the sunlight streaming through the kitchen window's curtains, so old that they were now see-through. "I hope you're hungry."

She nodded. "It smells great. Thank you."

He gave her a crooked smile full of promise as he cut and served the omelet, setting a plate and cutlery at their places. Rodelle took a bite, surprised by how much she had missed real food during their short trip. Eyeing her reaction, Brandon asked, "How is it? It would probably be a bit better with onions or garlic, but New Eden doesn't have either of them."

"Don't speak badly about this. It's delicious." She took another bite, chewing thoughtfully as she considered her next words. "We'll need our strength for later." She held her breath, waiting for his response.

He gave her a searing look that sent a bolt of heat straight through her. Rodelle knew that her earlier skittishness had been for nothing and now regretted not inviting him in the bath with her. It would have been a tight fit, but maybe, someday, she could figure out a way to install a shower unit, and . . .

"I like seeing you come out of your shell," he said. There was a rasp to his voice that hadn't been there before.

"I was thinking about . . . well, you know," she said. "The bathtub."

"What?"

He looked so thoroughly confused that she couldn't

help but laugh. "My bathroom. How there isn't enough room for two in the tub, but I could change that if there was a shower. I'm not sure how long I'll be staying in this house, though." She was babbling. "Don't mind me."

Brandon put down his fork. "Rodelle."

There was a serious note to his voice that hadn't been there before. "Yes?"

"You're not obligated to do anything you don't want to. We'll go as fast or slowly as you want."

She nodded. "I want everything with you. I think I have for a while." Color touched his cheeks at her admission, the sight sending an odd thrill through her. She liked having this kind of power over him, small as it was. She ate another mouthful of eggs, stalling. "I'm not good at this, is all."

"Is this an experience thing? Because I'm not exactly hopping from bed to bed, you know?"

Rodelle's gaze met his. "Really?"

"Relationship-wise," he added. "I'd rather not get into details, but we didn't all stay aboard the ship when it was docked for refueling at waystations. Some of us took in the sights, so to speak."

She nodded, understanding. "Got it."

Rodelle turned back to the remains of her meal, unsure what to do next. She wanted this man more than anything, yet she was stymied as to how to move forward. When she glanced at Brandon, he had a similarly perplexed expression on his face. Why the hell were both of them so shy after what had happened between them on their trip? "Is this so awkward because we're home?" she asked suddenly.

Brandon set down his tea. "I think so."

"Because when we were out there, I didn't feel like me." As she spoke the words, she felt like dawn had broken in her mind, casting light over emotions that she hadn't had terms for previously. "Like, I wasn't mousy little Rodelle Redfield Lansing, scared of her own shadow. I was someone who did something brave. Brave for me, anyway. For a few days, I was an intrepid explorer." She hadn't had the courage or knowledge to make contact with the cyborgs, like Hannah had, or jumped aboard their space-ship minutes before takeoff, like Jasmine. She thought about how heavy her share of their supplies had been on her back. "As intrepid as I can get without leaving New Eden."

"You've always been that person," Brandon said softly.

She shook her head. "No. I've always done what I was told to do, always been the obedient daughter and, later, wife, doing what was expected of me." Immediately, she wished she hadn't said "wife." It could bring the subject of Jackson to the discussion, which she wanted to avoid. She was trying to work up the nerve to jump on the man sitting across the table from her, a man she was actually attracted to.

A man who had gone out of his way to make her feel comfortable, who wanted her to feel like she was in control. Something in her relaxed a little at that realization. She drained the last of her tea and set aside the cup, steeling herself. Then she rose, crossing the short distance between them. Brandon shifted, turning his chair just enough so he could face her. Taking a deep breath, she bent down, taking his face into her hands, and kissed him, putting everything she could into it.

His response was immediate. He pulled her into his lap, arms tightening around her, tongue demanding entrance. Her breath caught, and a lightning-hot bolt of desire shot through her. His skin was hot under her touch, and the part of her brain still capable of rational thought wondered if hers was too. It certainly felt like it.

She shifted so she was straddling him, his thighs firm beneath her. Brandon let out a strangled noise from deep in his throat, his body flexing against hers. His erection pressed against her, a tease through their layers of clothing. Thin and threadbare as they may be, they were an impediment that Rodelle needed to get rid of. She reluctantly broke their kiss, pulling away from him just enough to take in the sight of him—breathless, eyes half-hooded with desire, lips swollen—and knew she had to look the same.

Heart thundering against her ribs, she reached for the hem of her tunic with shaking fingers. She ignored the wave of shyness that crested over her, reminding herself that he had seen her naked before, and likely with his eyes on night vision. The light in her kitchen had to be more flattering. She felt an irrational giggle rise and bit her lip to keep it inside.

"What is it?" Brandon asked, voice strained. He ran his hands over her body, still covered by her thin tunic. Her nipples poked at the fabric, and he lightly pinched one through it, drawing a squeak from her. She still held the hem in her fingers.

"Just—you've seen me in worse circumstances than this, and it didn't bother me." She fought back a smile, then dragged a finger across one of the metal components embedded in his skin.

"Does it bother you now?" He flexed under her again, his cock grinding against her. She gasped, wanting more.

"No, I just think it's funny that I'm wondering how I looked to you with your night vision on when I hadn't bathed in days, and now, well . . ." She held out her hands.

"Does this go back to your feeling like a different person when we were on the trip?"

"Yeah." She peeled away her tunic and tossed it away, not caring where it landed. His eyes widened. "I want to be her again. I want to be her always."

His hands cupped her face, urged her to his for a kiss. "You are," he murmured against her lips. "You always have been. It's what I liked about you right away."

A shiver of pleasure wracked her at his words. She was so unaccustomed to compliments that she received them like a parched garden finally being watered. "Thank you," she whispered.

"Mmm. It's the truth." His hand traveled down her back, then kneaded the soft flesh of her ass. She raised her head to look at him. "Tell me what happens next."

"What do you mean?"

"Are we doing this in the kitchen, or did you have somewhere else in mind?"

A crazy notion of riding him on the kitchen chair came to mind, an idea that Rodelle liked very much. It was quickly tempered by the realization that her chairs probably weren't strong enough to withstand that kind of activity. She clapped a hand over her mouth to keep from giggling. Goddamn it all, would she ever stop finding sexual things to laugh at?

At least Brandon looked amused, although, judging by the tension of his body under her, he was still aroused. "What is it?"

"I'd like to have sex with you in a chair sometime, but mine are too old. We'd fall on our asses."

She could tell he was trying not to laugh. "The bed it is, then." Without another word, he gripped her hips and stood up. She squealed in surprise, wrapping her arms around his shoulders. "Put your legs around me." Rodelle was only too happy to oblige.

He carried her through the small house, to her long-disused bedroom. For once, the sight of her bed didn't fill her with dread. Excitement welled in her, and with it, more ideas. "Can you throw me on the bed?" she asked. "Not with your full strength, but enough so I know you can't wait for this."

He looked at her like she was nuts. "I *can't* wait. I've been waiting for this for weeks."

"So, do it."

His dark brows lifted in amusement. "As you wish."

She fell on her back, cushioned by the straw-and-rag-filled mattress. A thrill coursed through her as he followed, crawling up the bed to cage her with his body, his hands bracing on either side of her head. He'd thrown away his towel, or it had fallen away and she hadn't noticed. How the hell had she not? Brandon was magnificent.

His cock pressed against her hip, a tantalizing reminder of what was going to happen. She traced a finger over his chest, dragging it along his skin and the metal pieces there. There was a fine web of white scars around one piece embedded in his breastbone. He sucked in a harsh breath as her hand traveled lower, finally wrapping around his erection and lightly stroking it. "If you keep doing that, this will be over before it's begun," he warned her.

That she had that kind of power over him was heady. She let go with some reluctance.

With a metallic sparkle in his eyes, he kissed a path from her lips down her throat, past her breastbone and down her belly. He gently urged her legs apart before his mouth found her pussy in a motion that nearly had her bucking off the bed. Her hands gripping his hair, she bit back a strangled cry of pleasure.

He raised his head. "Should I stop?"

"No!"

He grinned. "Good. I've wanted to do this for a while." He ducked his head again, his tongue teasing her before finding her clit. Another cry escaped her. Encouraged, he slid one of his hands from its spot under her thigh, his finger gently pushing into her, then withdrawing. Rodelle's hips bucked against him again of their own volition, and he added a second finger. Lifting his head so his gaze could meet hers, his eyes never left her face as he pumped his fingers inside her.

She shifted against him, needing more, but not wanting everything to be over yet. "Brandon," she said, her voice soft but urgent. "I need . . ."

"I know. So do I." To her surprise and disappointment, he pulled his fingers out of her and kissed her knee. Crawling off the bed, he said, "I'll be right back." Then he left the room.

What the hell?

He returned a few seconds later, a small bottle of something wheat-colored and viscous in his hand. "Oil," he said at her quizzical expression.

"Oh!" She hadn't thought of that. "Thank you."

"You shouldn't have to feel obligated to thank me for thinking about your comfort, sweetheart," he murmured.

An odd, unfamiliar feeling swept through her at being called that. Rodelle couldn't recall ever having an affectionate nickname before.

He settled back on the bed next to her, leaving the bottle on the floor. "It's body safe," he explained.

"What's it usually meant for?" she couldn't help but ask.

"Cooking, but it's multi-functional." He brushed a strand of hair out of her eyes. "What happens next, Rodelle? What do you want?"

A low thrum of desire coursed through her, and with it,

half a dozen fantasies she had secretly harbored since meeting him. "I want to ride you."

That devilish grin split his face again. "I was hoping you'd say that." He reached for the oil, spreading some on his hands. He stroked his erection, his body straining a little. "Come here."

She was only too happy to comply.

Straddling his hips, she grasped his cock, guiding it into her as she lowered herself on his body. It took a few seconds for her to adjust to his size, taking deep breaths until he was fully seated inside her. Hands braced against his chest, she wiggled her hips experimentally, a motion that coaxed a groan of pleasure from him.

"This is even better than I thought it would be," he ground out. He gripped her hips and thrust into her, as if illustrating his point.

Rodelle slid up on him, then let herself fall, crying out as she did so. Drawing herself up on her knees again, she repeated the motion, not breaking eye contact with Brandon.

"Do it," he said, his voice a strained whisper. "I want to see you ride me and come around me."

His words alone were almost enough to bring her to orgasm. *Almost.*

She didn't know who moved first, only that their bodies worked in perfect rhythm, as though they were made for each other. Brandon's earlier warning about how he wouldn't last long echoed in her mind as she rode him, encouraged by his low moans and fingers greedily digging into her hips as he thrust into her and withdrew in a pattern that already had her on edge. She bore down on him, desperate to come as he'd ordered her to, bolstered by his increasing speed that told her he was close too.

His expression was glazed, body tense beneath her as

she came, her cry muffled when she bit into his shoulder. She fell against his chest as he continued thrusting in her, cock swelling as his own orgasm ripped through him, her name on his lips.

A creak sounded beneath them, and the bed gave way as its legs collapsed. Still inside her, Brandon didn't let her go as they slid to the side.

For a few seconds, the only sound in the room was of their breathing. Rodelle lifted her head, stunned to see that they'd broken the bed. "Oh, my God," she muttered.

It took a few seconds for Brandon to catch his breath. "No shit." He pressed a kiss to her forehead, then gently eased out of her before wrapping her in a hug. "When can we do that again?"

CHAPTER TEN

RODELLE LOOKED PEACEFUL IN SLEEP, her breaths deep and even. Not wanting to wake her, Brandon slipped out of bed as quietly as he could, then tucked the sheet around her. She stirred but didn't wake. He couldn't help but smile when he looked at the bed, now bereft of its remaining legs after he'd popped them off after it partially collapsed.

His backup energy reserves would keep him going for another thirty-two hours if he wanted, giving him ample opportunity to find out if his brethren had discovered anything on the clearscreens they'd brought back. Guilt twinged at him when he thought of them working while he'd been having fun, but it disappeared when he reminded himself that any one of them would have done the same thing in his situation. *Except Rhys,* he thought wryly. *Hannah too.* Both of them were devoted to the betterment of their societies in ways no one else was.

After a quick bath and cup of coffee, he set off from the house to the ship. The settlement seemed more vibrant in the afternoon, with more people out and about than he could remember before. Belatedly, he remembered the arrival of the Si'laar, then the allegations of their previous clones stealing the Si'laar ship and tech. Some of his good mood vanished. Between the Si'laar appearance, the clearscreens discovery, and James's reappearance and poor health, he had run away from a lot in favor of spending a morning in bed.

The exterior ramp to the cyborgs' cruiser was still extended when he arrived, the airlock and cargo bays open. Dimly, he could hear the noises of the livestock from their new homes in the agri-center, likely one of the reasons for New Eden's heightened spirits. Brandon made a mental note to take a look at the barn, see what would be on a menu someday soon.

He strode up the ramp and through the airlock. His vision immediately adjusted to the relative dimness inside, and the familiar, faint buzz of the ship's systems traveled through him as his cybernetics recognized where he was. Brandon connected to the ship, the craft's crew locator telling him that CW44 and James were aboard, in the sickbay. His gut twisted as he remembered Rodelle's friend and his likely diagnosis.

It had been hours since CW44 and James disappeared into the sickbay. What exactly was wrong with James that couldn't be cured with the considerable equipment on board in half an hour's time?

Brandon didn't bother trying to contact CW44 via their shared link, not wanting to disturb his fellow cyborg, should he be doing something medical and messy. Instead, he headed for the sickbay, descending stairs until he reached it. He was surprised to see the door was wide open, James sitting on one of the three beds in it, his back to Brandon. CW44 stood in front of him but looked up when Brandon appeared in the doorway. "He graces us with his presence," he said by way of greeting, his tone deadpan. His eyes glowed brightly, and he held a suture pen in one hand, the sight of which was alarming to Brandon. What the hell had he done to James?

Brandon ignored the quip. "How is everything going?"

"Mr. Thierry is not going to die," CW44 said. He set aside his suture pen, straightened his shoulders, and blinked. His dark eyes returned to their normal hue.

"Well, we all die, but I'm not dying from this," James said, a little too cheerfully for someone who had just undergone something invasive, if he was being stitched up. He twisted around to grin at Brandon. His face was still freckled and sunburnt, his overgrown red hair tangled, but there was something different about his face compared to this morning. Yet the metallic glint in his left eye was oddly familiar . . .

Brandon took a half-step back with an undignified yelp. "What the fuck? You gave him a cybernetic eye?"

James gave a weird half-laugh at Brandon's reaction. CW44 scowled. "I also removed two epidermal carcinomas. I just finished closing the wound on the second."

"He's good," said James appreciatively. A muscle ticked in CW44's jaw at the compliment, his expression unreadable.

"I can't believe you gave him a cybernetic eye!"

CW44's gaze was steely. "Was I supposed to give him chicken soup and hope it would keep the cancer from spreading? Isn't that your domain?"

"Brandon doesn't seem the type to let cancer spread," said James.

"I was referring to his culinary leanings."

"Oh, wow. You can make chicken soup from scratch?" James gave Brandon an appreciative look.

"Theoretically, but Hannah might kill me if I did anything to one of the chickens right now." Brandon scrubbed a hand over his face. "I just can't believe you took out James's eye."

"It was easier to replace it with something that's malignancy-proof, rather than cloning a new one." CW44 shrugged. "He was a good patient."

"He gave me some good drugs to knock me out," James added with more enthusiasm than Brandon would have expected.

"I should hope so." Brandon leaned against an empty bed. "I can't believe you did three surgeries in one morning."

"Plus the aliens," said James. "I'm going to visit them when they come out tonight, see what they're up to. You picked a really good time to bring me back to the settlement."

"Technically, I performed one surgery and two excisions, both of which are well within my scope of practice." CW44 eyed Brandon suspiciously. "Where have you been, anyway?"

"I went home. Rodelle was tired." Eventually.

James's eye had a twinkle in it that had nothing to do with its cybernetics. "I bet."

CW44 sighed. "I wish I hadn't asked." To James, he said, "We were interrupted at a decent time. You are free from cancer cells now. Going forward, do not sunbathe nude. I would advise against doing that, even if you weren't prone to cancer the way you are. Your diet must also change."

"Yeah, no shit. You took me away from my crabs."

"Eat more vegetables. There are plenty in New Eden now. And wear a hat when you go outside. I can make one for you if you don't have one at home."

"Oh, I don't have a home right now. It fell down in the

quake. I checked," James said casually, as if that wasn't awful.

Something softened in CW44's expression for a half-second, so fast that Brandon nearly missed it. "I'm certain that can be remedied soon."

"I don't mind sleeping outside," James insisted.

"I do. Technically, you are convalescing. You cannot do that sleeping in the grass. And remember what I said about the gene therapy, when we have the equipment necessary to do that."

"I'll be a robot man, like you." James looked intrigued at the prospect. Alarm flared through Brandon. What the hell had CW44 promised him?

Something must have shown on Brandon's face, because CW44 explained, "Mr. Thierry has a recessive genetic mutation that predisposes him to certain cancers."

"Oh, shit," said Brandon.

"They can be corrected with genetic therapy. I can treat James for it when the hospital has been built."

"I didn't even know that was a thing," Brandon replied.

"They're rare, but they occasionally appear in humans with ancestry in certain parts of the galaxy. I am confident that I have removed all malignant cells for the time being and can prevent further cancers from developing." To James, he said, "You can go now. Speak to Hannah to see if she knows of an empty house you can stay in for the time being."

James's head bobbed up and down in agreement. "Yeah, she'll know. I guess she's running things now that Jackson's gone?"

Brandon stiffened at the mention of Rodelle's dead husband. "I suppose so."

"Yeah. Fucking incredible, the stuff she's done."

Brandon nearly agreed, then realized James was still talking about Hannah. He nodded.

"Speaking of fucking incredible things, a few of our brethren have been looking at the clearscreens we brought back," said CW44 pointedly.

In his haste to see if James was all right, Brandon had forgotten about the clearscreens. "What did they find?" he asked.

"I've been dipping in and out of the shared link. I gathered that much of the data consists of old star charts, routes that haven't been in use for centuries and don't appear on modern charts. It lends credence to the theory that the original New Edeners were involved in illicit activity."

"I can't believe you can talk to each other telepathically," James said in awe.

"I can't believe he was doing it while operating on you," Brandon added.

CW44's reply was indignant. "I did no such thing. It was between treatments, and I don't have to parse a star chart to know what it is. I haven't asked about the specifics."

"Wait. You said the star charts were centuries old," said Brandon, thinking. "Of course they would be. The New Eden colony was established over a century ago."

"These charts predated their arrival. They haven't been used for at least two, three hundred years. That's indicative of a population that was well-versed in space travel and navigation. Hardly the hallmarks of a people determined to live in self-sufficiency and ignorant of technology." CW44 looked at James again. "You, go find somewhere to live. I'm going to speak to the others about the clearscreens."

"What about the aliens?" James asked, unperturbed by the order.

"The Si'laar's appearance is beyond my intellectual or emotional capacity at the moment."

James's only reply to that statement was a blank stare.

Sighing, the other cyborg explained, "I do not have the mental energy to consider the newest immigrants to New Eden right now, in addition to the latest revelations about your forebears."

"Oh." James slid off the bed. "I guess I'll see you later." With a wave to Brandon, he left the sickbay.

"Does he know how to get out of the ship?" Brandon asked CW44 when he left.

"I'm certain he can retrace his steps. He cheerfully pointed out every landmark he could on the way here. He didn't stop talking until I sedated him." Faint disdain crossed CW44's expression.

Brandon bit back a smile.

"I would expect a hermit to be quieter." CW44 nodded his head to the door. "Let me clean up here, then I'll join the others above deck working on the clearscreens. I'll meet you there."

Brandon knew when he was being dismissed. The other cyborg had always kept to himself, preferring to communicate via their shared link and only using his physical voice when they arrived on New Eden. It was a sharp contrast to Brandon, who had been delighted to have the opportunity to live as a normal man and would happily forget how to use the link altogether if he could.

Brandon found a few of his fellow cyborgs on the ship's bridge. While a couple of them pored over the clearscreens themselves, others had cables snaking from ports in their wrists and backs of the hands, the devices physically plugged into them. Darius was one of the latter, his eyes blank as he processed data. Brandon nearly made a quip about his brain's computer not having enough space to accommodate it and the serial episodes he was fond of but refrained, not wanting to distract him. TM34—Tommy now—was in a similar state, frozen in place as exabytes of data flowed into his brain. Rhys and Aiden, formerly AL16, looked up from the clearscreens in their hands, Rhys nodding in acknowledgement. "Good to finally see you," Rhys said.

"Is that a dig about my getting some rest after coming home from a multi-day trip that had me bring these and a missing New Edener back?"

Darius laughed aloud. He blinked and his eyes went back to normal, irises returning to their dark brown shade. "Resting? You're so full of shit."

Rhys blinked in confusion but didn't prod. "There's more to look for in the north on another trip, but you did bring back a great deal of useful information."

"Glad to know I'm good for something."

"Come on, you make great doughnuts and roasted naroki," Darius said.

"How do you know about the doughnuts?" Brandon asked.

Darius looked at him like he was malfunctioning. "Jasmine told me."

"Hannah told me about them," Rhys added. "Fried desserts are a novelty here."

Aiden pulled a cable from his wrist. His eyes returned to their normal dark brown hue. "The original New Edeners were low-level employees of a now-defunct criminal empire who double-crossed their bosses and set up a sanctuary here to escape them."

The abrupt change in subject nearly had Brandon's

head spinning. They had suspected as much, but to have it confirmed was a hell of a thing. "What?"

He felt slight pressure at the back of his skull, a sign that Aiden was trying to communicate with him over their link. Brandon tripped the code in his brain to link in and was immediately flooded with data. As CW44 had said before, a great deal of it was old star charts, used to circumvent the criminals the original New Edeners had escaped from after—

Brandon concentrated, looking for the reason for their flight but couldn't find it. "What the hell did they steal?" he muttered to himself.

"Money is my best guess," Aiden said.

Quiet footsteps sounded behind Brandon, and with it, a faint antiseptic odor. He didn't have to turn around to know it was CW44. "What a perverse thing to be motivated by," CW44 muttered.

"Exact details of the heist could be on other data sources in the north," Rhys said. "Or they could be lost to time. The important thing is we now know the original settlers' true motivations—they were on the run from dangerous people."

"And our previous iterations did business with some of them," Aiden added.

"Which could partly explain why our ship was able to pick up the SOS from Hannah in the first place, if the ship still had the comms tower's origin codes in its databanks," said Brandon. He was probably the least technically inclined cyborg in their group, but even he knew that. "Is there anything in the clearscreen data about those transactions?"

Rhys shook his head. "No, but there is data pertaining to livestock and building supplies being delivered in exchange for water, which New Eden has in abundance. It stands to reason that our previous iterations found that a reasonable trade."

It made sense. Fresh water reserves were expensive in remote areas of space. In others, water was both expensive and subject to outrageous taxes. It provided a measure of relief to Brandon that, at least, their previous clones hadn't mounted an attack against New Eden.

CW44 cleared his throat. "Speaking of water, what are we to do about the Si'laar?"

Brandon nearly pointed out that CW44 had dismissed all thoughts of the Si'laar only minutes ago, but refrained, not wanting to pick an argument. Instead, he racked his brain, trying to remember the details about the newest additions to New Eden. He'd been in a bit of a hurry to get back to the house with Rodelle when they returned to the settlement.

"They're a water-dwelling species," CW44 added. "I took the liberty of conducting some research on them when we returned."

"While you were operating on James?" Brandon asked, aghast. "I thought you were out of patience for new information."

CW44's response was terse. "No, before. It took about four seconds to find a short summary of their species in the ship's archives, perhaps three paragraphs. They're nearly extinct."

Brandon's brief elation that the cyborgs' previous clones hadn't slaughtered New Edeners evaporated. Their ship was modified Si'laar tech. Had they helped contribute to the Si'laar extinction when they'd acquired it? The notion was sickening.

"We will be meeting with them later tonight, when it's safer for them to come outside," Rhys explained. "I'm certain this is one meeting at the amphitheater that won't cause too much grumbling."

CW44 made a noncommittal noise. Darius and Aiden exchanged a look that said they didn't believe Rhys.

Rhys began collecting the clearscreens. "I'll upload the data to a readable format accessible to everyone," he said. "At least we know New Eden's true origins and that the settlers and our clones likely weren't violent, at least after a couple of generations."

"There would be a record of mass violence," Aiden piped up. "Told to each new generation as a cautionary tale against contacting the rest of the galaxy. Pauline has told me a great deal of New Eden's history as best she could, and there is nothing of that scenario in her stories."

It took Brandon a few seconds to remember who he was talking about. A quiet woman, living alone on the side of the settlement opposite him and Rodelle, closer to where Darius, Simon, and Jasmine shared a house. If memory served him correctly, Pauline and Aiden had taken up a relationship together almost immediately, the first to do so.

"That's a positive thing to know," Rhys said. To CW44, he asked, "How is your patient?"

CW444 blinked in surprise at the change of subject. "Mr. Thierry has a genetic mutation that must be treated as soon as possible. I have replaced his eye with a cybernetically enhanced one and removed two carcinomas from his skin."

"Excellent work. And his mental health?" Rhys prodded.

CW44 hesitated for a couple of seconds. "That's outside my scope of practice."

"The brain is an organ in the body. Is he despondent or anxious?"

"The non-stop chattering could be a sign of anxiety, but I would have to spend more time with him to be certain." A shadow crossed CW44's face at the notion.

"Perhaps you should," Rhys said.

CW44's eyes widened. "What?"

"A New Edener with cancer and lacking all social interactions for a period of years is bound to have some emotional and mental issues to work through," said Darius. "We'll all keep an eye on him. Jasmine was beside herself when she found out he was alive."

"Hannah too," said Rhys. "CW44, how are your physical faculties?"

"I would like to go to bed early tonight, but I have thirteen hours of energy reserves to sustain me for now, if needed."

Rhys nodded. "Excellent. Take a look in the cargo holds and help out the others there. They brought back a hospital's worth of supplies and equipment. With your help, the medical facility can be completed by the end of the day."

CW44 brightened at the mention of the hospital. "Of course."

To the rest of them, Rhys said, "We all have to help put up the pre-fab homes. They are designed to withstand frequent seismic activity. We have supplies to build ten houses so far."

That was promising. Brandon followed the rest of the cyborgs out of the bridge and through the ship. Stepping into the sunlight, he thought of Rodelle, of their chance to build something great.

CHAPTER ELEVEN

IT WAS late afternoon when Rodelle woke alone in bed, the first time she had slept in it since the earthquake. As she washed and dressed, she thought about how drastically her perception of the house had changed in only a few short hours. Dread at its bad memories didn't crawl down her spine like an insect as she padded through the short hallway to the kitchen, where she pumped some water into a mug. When she finished it, she drank another cup, noting the humidity closing in on her, something she had forgotten about since her move into the guesthouse, with its open window. She supposed she was moving back into the main house.

Brandon was gone, which wasn't a surprise. A flicker of guilt twinged through her when she thought about how she had whiled away half the day getting caught up on sleep after their unexpected—yet entirely welcome and needed—lovemaking that morning. The feeling only intensified when she remembered James's grim diagnosis and the appearance of the Si'laar.

She had drained her cup again when a knock sounded

at the door. "Be right there!" she called, hurrying through the house.

Hannah and Jasmine waited for her on the other side. "There you are," said Hannah. "You weren't in the guesthouse."

Rodelle felt herself color. "I've decided to move back in."

Jasmine grinned, giving her a knowing look, and Rodelle felt her blush deepen. "With Brandon?"

"Yes." There was no point in obfuscating it. She held the door open. "Come on in. I'm afraid I don't have much in the way of refreshments to offer you this afternoon. We haven't had a chance to bake anything."

Jasmine chortled, while Hannah hid a smile behind her hand. "I'll bet," said Jasmine. Rodelle closed the door behind them.

"Has anything else happened while I was sleeping?" Rodelle asked. "Another alien delegation arriving, maybe?"

"No, and the Si'laar are still on board their ship, recharging or something. I'm not sure," Hannah replied. "We're going to have a meeting later tonight, when it's safe for them to be outside. It seems they don't do well in sunlight."

"And they chose to come to New Eden, where we have two suns?" In the kitchen, Rodelle looked around for something to serve her friends. Despite her apologies for not having anything suitable for snacking, she did find a few ripe tomatoes. She sliced them while Hannah and Jasmine took seats at the table, then sprinkled the pieces with a powdered seasoning brought back from the nearest waystation.

"We'll get specifics later, I'm sure." Hannah helped herself to a tomato piece and tasted it. "Wow, this is good. They need a place to stay, just like the cyborgs did, and would prefer to live in freshwater, like they're supposed to. God knows we have plenty of it."

"So, they'll live in the sea?" Rodelle asked.

Hannah nodded. "At least, during the daytime, if I'm understanding that right. They prefer to spend days in the water and nights on the land."

"They aren't even mad about the cyborgs stealing their ship back in the day," Jasmine added, then tasted a tomato slice. "You're right, this is good. What's on it?"

"A blended seasoning. I'm not sure what the exact ingredients are," Rodelle replied.

"Have you seen Brandon?" Hannah asked.

"Not since this morning."

"So, then, he hasn't told you what was on those screen things you brought back from the north."

Damn it, she'd nearly forgotten about them—the whole point of the trip in the first place. Her heartbeat picked up speed. "No. What was on them?"

"Rhys said it was all maps and logs, evidence that the original New Edeners were criminals. Probably low-level thugs who pissed off their bosses, then fled here with their families to escape them." Hannah's answer was delivered as casually as if she was talking about the weather.

Rodelle leaned back in her chair, relieved. They had suspected something along those lines, anyway. "I see."

"It doesn't look like the organization they worked for has existed for decades, anyway, so it's unlikely that anyone will come all the way here to exact revenge. Even the business they did with previous cyborg clones wasn't that bad. They delivered supplies from off-world in exchange for water, according to Rhys. Nothing too horrible." Hannah helped herself to another piece of tomato. Jasmine did likewise.

"So, we're descended from people who ran away from

the law and mobsters, not rugged individualists," Rodelle said. "It makes a lot more sense."

Jasmine nodded. "They could have been both. It explains why we had little things, like holographs and spools of thread. There was no way the original settlers prioritized those kinds of things when they made their plans for this place." She finished her tomato slice and reached for another. Before she could bite into it, she added, "Rhys was talking about another trip to the north to get the rest of what's in the caves. They brought back an anti-grav flitter on the last supply run, so it will only take a day or two, at the most."

"What's a flitter?" Rodelle asked.

"It's a ground vehicle," Hannah replied excitedly. She and Jasmine exchanged a look, grins on their faces. "We even got to drive it for a few minutes."

Jealousy flared in Rodelle. "That sounds like fun."

"It was!" said Jasmine.

"Until we tipped it over." Hannah helped herself to more tomato.

"We're okay," said Jasmine. "It righted itself as soon as it leaned over. But we're not allowed to drive it again until Rhys has given us some lessons."

"Or when the hospital's been finished, whichever comes first," said Hannah. "I thought Rhys's heart would give out when it tilted. Anyway, I think I'd like to go to the north sometime. Rhys is going, and CW44 wants to return too."

"You want a chance to drive the flitter again," said Jasmine.

"Yeah, no shit, I want to drive the flitter again. That thing is fun."

"What about you?" Rodelle asked Jasmine. "Do you want to go to the north too?"

Jasmine waved her hand dismissively. "Maybe some other time. If I went, I'd like to go with Simon and Darius on a camping trip alone."

"The camping isn't too bad. Just be careful of the river," Rodelle warned. "I face planted in it."

"I've never really camped before, so I have nothing to compare it to," said Jasmine. "We might not even go as far as you did. Maybe just to that weird grassy field James said is outside the settlement. That seems far enough for me."

"Far enough for what?" Hannah asked.

"So no one will hear us."

Rodelle laughed, and Hannah blushed. "You don't even want to see the sea in the north?" Rodelle asked. "It's beautiful."

"Maybe if another flitter for everyone's use is available. I'm just enjoying building a home with my guys, you know?"

Rodelle was beginning to understand that feeling. "Yes."

"Speaking of homes, James is staying with Ollie until we can get the first round of pre-fab houses built," said Hannah.

Rodelle blinked in surprise. "Ollie agreed to this?"

"It was Ollie's idea. He's his second or third cousin or something, I'm not sure. The Wests and Thierrys go way back."

"It's probably a good thing that we have to think about how people are related," said Jasmine. "I think New Eden did pretty well at avoiding inbreeding, at least."

"The only good thing they did," Rodelle agreed.

"That reminds me of something I was thinking about," said Hannah.

Jasmine raised a pale eyebrow. "You were thinking about inbreeding?"

"Yeah, sort of. There were over a hundred settlers in the beginning. Were all of them on the run from this criminal syndicate? That seems like a shitload of fugitives."

Rodelle considered this new angle. "Maybe only some of them were criminals, and they duped innocent people into joining the colony. Conned them out of their money for supplies, that kind of thing."

"That seems the likeliest scenario right now." Hannah rose and opened one of the cupboards, removing an earthenware mug. "Are any of you thirsty?"

"I could go for some water," said Jasmine.

Hannah's hand hovered over the sink's water pump handle. She paused, then picked up a paper-wrapped tea cube. "What's this?"

"Tea and coffee cubes from the last supply run."

Jasmine's eyes widened, taking on a nearly feral look. "You have coffee?"

"Yeah. Do you want some?"

"Oh, my God, yes!" Jasmine was out of her seat faster than Rodelle had ever seen her move. "I haven't had any since our trip to the waystation!" She switched on the kettle and pulled out a mug of her own from the cupboard. "Han, do you want any?"

Hannah still held the tea cube. "Can I try this instead? It smells good."

"Sure," said Rodelle.

Hannah peeled back the paper wrapping. "Am I supposed to drink it hot or cold?"

"Either," replied Jasmine. "Iced tea is mentioned a lot in one of the books I'm reading right now."

"I don't have any ice," Rodelle replied.

"Well, cold tea, then." The kettle let out a tinny whine as it came to a boil. Jasmine dropped a coffee cube in her cup, then poured water over it. She brought it to her nose and inhaled, a blissful look on her face. "Brandon won't mind that we had some of his stash?"

"No. He's talked about planting coffee and tea bushes, in fact."

"Do tea and coffee grow on bushes?" Hannah pumped water into a cup, then added the tea cube. She stirred it with a metal spoon.

"I'm actually not sure," Rodelle replied. "Maybe some kinds do?"

Hannah took a cautious sip of her drink. Her dark brows raised in surprise. "Much better than dandelion tea, I can tell you that."

"It's the caffeine," said Jasmine.

Hannah looked at her blankly.

"It's the stimulant in coffee and tea."

"Oh." Hannah took another swallow. "I like it."

"Oh, yeah, I was hooked the first time I tried it on the ship." Jasmine blew on her cup, then tasted it. "Rodelle, I assume you're going to the meeting at the amphitheater tonight?"

"I wouldn't miss it for the world."

"That has to be the first time in New Eden history that someone has said that about a meeting," Hannah pointed out.

"No, we were all pretty eager to go to the first one with the cyborgs," Jasmine said.

Rodelle recalled that, as well as the undercurrent of fear that had rippled through New Eden the night the cyborgs landed in their untended field. She still remembered the noise, the people outside rushing to see what had happened, how she was ripped from a fitful sleep fraught with nightmares of the quake. Of Jackson's enraged expression as he lay crushed under a support column of the collapsed community center, his voice reduced to an angry, hoarse stage whisper, ordering her to save him through blood-flecked lips. Of his threats to make her sorry that she didn't help.

She'd helped, in the end. But not in a way that benefited Jackson, nor one that she could ever speak about.

"Rodelle?" Hannah's voice snapped her out of her memories.

She blinked, trying to clear her mind of the memories that she had kept hidden so well since she became friendly with Brandon. He—along with Hannah and Jasmine—would think her a monster if they ever found out what really happened to Jackson the night of the quake. At least she didn't feel tears pricking at her eyes. If she had, she might have broken down and told her friends everything. "I'm good," she said brightly. "Just thinking, is all."

Hannah pinned her with a stare for a few seconds. "You kind of zoned out there. Jasmine was saying that James now has a cybernetic eye. Did you know he was getting that?"

"He lost his eye?" Rodelle hadn't been expecting that to be a treatment for James's illness.

"Yeah, he had cancer. He said CW44 told him he would need more preventative treatment once the hospital is completed." Hannah's brow scrunched in confusion. "He seems awfully chipper for someone who had a body part cut out of him."

"Yeah, he was chipper the whole trip back to the settlement."

Hannah shook her head. "He isn't okay. I'm glad he's back, but he's not okay, and I don't mean with his cancer." She paused. "The cancer and his genes can be treated, at least. I'm not sure how yet. James said the anesthetic was awesome and he can now do close-ups with his new eye, whatever that means."

Rodelle was inclined to agree. "He'll fit right in again."

Hannah and Jasmine were quiet, waiting for her to explain.

She sighed. "Well, none of us are fully okay yet, are we?"

CHAPTER TWELVE

THE SUNSET LEFT the sky streaked with pink and orange, a beacon to New Eden to make their way to the amphitheater. Rodelle felt oddly relaxed as she ambled to the dilapidated gathering place.

The waning light from the twin suns bounced off the light-colored roofs of the newly built prefabricated houses and small hospital as she walked by, the structures constructed in a few short hours. Rodelle had watched a house go up, and it was truly incredible—a wide, flat box would be hauled from the belly of the cyborgs' ship on an anti-grav pallet, then a cyborg would press a few buttons on the top. The box unfolded itself, assembling a frame in a matter of minutes before separate walls and roof from the bottom of the box were raised and pressed into place. The first time Rodelle had seen it happen, she seriously considered that she might be dreaming or at least hallucinating from the stress of the last few days. But no, there really were new houses here, and more homes to come.

The new hospital stood in the same place as the old clinic once did, its sides colored blue beneath a cream-colored roof. The new structures were made of a material that was unfamiliar to Rodelle, something synthetic that felt like wood but wasn't. Almost like the plastic dishware from the old world that was still used in some houses, but with an odd, brick-like texture.

She met James on the path to the amphitheater, surprised to see his overgrown reddish hair clipped close to this scalp. He bounded over to her the way Rodelle imagined a puppy might, a wide smile on his face. "I just had some genetic therapy," he announced.

"Is that why your hair is missing?"

"Oh, yeah." He touched his shorn hair at the reminder. "Sort of. I felt like I should cut it, you know? Connor helped me at the hospital."

"Who's Connor?"

"That's what I'm calling CW now."

Rodelle was slightly taken aback to hear that. "He picked another name?"

James shrugged, unaware of what a monumental decision that could be for the cyborgs. "I asked about how cyborg names work, you know, with the initials and numbers."

"It's the initials of their originals and the number of their clone."

He gave her an exasperated look. "Yeah, I know that now. Anyway, he said he was thinking of picking a new name, and I asked if he wanted any help and just listed off a bunch of names that start with C. I guess I had too many ideas because after I said 'Connor,' he said he'd had enough and Connor was good enough for him."

Rodelle snorted, then covered her mouth with her hand to stifle her laugh at the image. "At least he made sure your genes work normally now." She considered her words for a second. "Is that the correct term?"

"I mean, it describes what's been fixed, so I guess so."

"What did he do?"

"He froze the skin on my arm and used this metal thing like an old-timey ink pen from the old world to inject something in me. He said it was like a nanobot, I think, that rewrites DNA and corrects the broken piece that predisposes me to skin and eye cancers. I'm missing a few of the right medical terms, but that's the gist of it."

"And he cut your hair."

"Well, I cut it, and he helped. The hospital's the only place I could find scissors, and I needed help with the back." He looked ahead of them, at the path that would take them to the amphitheater. "Do you think it's rude to call the Si'laar aliens? We're the aliens to them, right?"

"I guess so." Any other explanation Rodelle could have offered left her mind when she saw Brandon approaching them. Her worry over the Si'laar's appearance lifted a little when she saw how relaxed he looked, like everything was going to be okay. Maybe it would be. If the Si'laar were out for revenge, wouldn't they have struck New Eden without warning? Why ask for their help, instead of taking what they needed?

Brandon laced his fingers through hers and leaned down to kiss her, in full view of everyone present. She couldn't help the shiver of pleasure that raced down her spine at the contact, the public acknowledgement of his affection. "Hi," she said, her voice coming out breathier than she'd intended.

"I missed you." His voice was soft, sincere. Looking over her shoulder at James, he asked, "How are you feeling?"

"Pretty good. My new eye is amazing." As if he could demonstrate his new organ's abilities, his eyes widened, and he looked around the area. His new eye was a lighter blue than his original one and had a telltale metallic glint to it. Fixing his gaze on Rodelle, he said, "I can count your eyebrow hairs if you want."

"Can *you* count my eyebrow hairs?" Rodelle asked Brandon.

"If I focused like James is, yes. I prefer to keep my vision on normal humanoid mode."

James blinked. "How do I make it go back to normal?"

Brandon opened his mouth to reply, then closed it without a word. It took a few seconds for him to say, "I just think about it, to be honest."

"Oh." James blinked again. "Okay, there it goes. Weird. It'll take a while to get used to it. My vision magnifies when it wants to."

Hannah, Rhys, and one of the Si'laar were waiting on the amphitheater stage when they arrived. The Si'laar's long robe had been replaced with a loose gray shipsuit, revealing a slender body of indeterminate sex, their four arms . . . Now it was Rodelle's turn to blink. She'd only spotted two on their bodies when they wore their long, hooded robes. The second pair of arms was shorter, extending from the middle of their torso. Two pairs of four-fingered hands, the backs covered in large scales, were clasped at their front. A single thick, white eyebrow rose in an arc over a pair of light eyes the color of a storm cloud, matching the short puff of white hair on their head. Their hair looked damp, as if they'd just emerged from the water. They probably had.

Hannah sat on the stage, her legs dangling over the edge. She spoke animatedly to a few people gathered around, introducing the Si'laar to them. The Si'laar bowed his head in greeting to each.

To the side was Rhys, speaking to another Si'laar who still wore their robe, the hood now lowered. Their white hair was longer than the one Hannah chatted with, flowing down their back, their single eyebrow bushier. For half a second, Rodelle wondered if James was counting their hairs. Rhys and the Si'laar looked like they were having some difficulties communicating, judging by the hand gestures of each and Rhys's obvious struggle not to speak louder in an attempt to get his point across.

Hannah caught Rodelle's eye and waved with a wide smile. Rodelle waved back, then took a seat at a nearby wooden bench, its surface worn smooth from decades of use. Brandon and James sat on either side of her.

"Rodelle!"

She didn't have to turn around to know the voice was Jasmine's. But she did, to say hello to her friend, who was flanked on either side by her cyborg boyfriends. They sat on the bench behind Rodelle's.

To James, Jasmine asked, "How are you? I know that's a stupid question, but good manners dictate that I should ask."

"I have a new eye."

"Yeah, I heard. Word travels fast. I guess you were the first patient at the new hospital?" She grinned. "Holy shit, I can't believe we have a *hospital* now!"

Rodelle hadn't had time to fully absorb that bit of news. The realization hit her with the force of a ton of bricks. *Like the ones that fell on Jackson.* Her elation turned to ice water in her veins, and she felt her smile falter. Why the hell did she have to think about him—of her role in his death—now, of all times? *Fuck!* Quickly recovering, she said, "I can hardly believe it!" To James, she added, "I can't believe you're back with us too!"

Jasmine tilted her head to the side, expression quizzical, and Rodelle wondered what her friend was thinking about. A second later, her glee returned. To James, she said, "You picked a good time to come back."

"Oh, I didn't choose to come back. They all but forced me to." Despite the gravity of that statement, James still sounded cheerful. "This is leagues better than the New Eden I walked away from, you know? If . . ."

He was cut off by Hannah standing and calling the meeting to order. "First of all, thank you for coming and not being irritated by this." A couple of people offered nervous laughter in response. "A lot has happened over the last couple of days, and I'm glad we can talk about this." She looked back at Rhys, who now stood next to the pair of Si'laar. The robed one's hands had disappeared into the garment. Rhys nodded in encouragement, offering her one of his rare smiles. "I'm not sure where I should even start," Hannah admitted. She looked a little flustered, very unlike the Hannah Rodelle everyone knew so well. "I guess with the Si'laar. I think we still have some negotiations to sort through, but the remaining Si'laar will be staying on New Eden permanently, establishing a daytime colony in the sea on the west side."

"New neighbors," said Jasmine quietly, excitement in her voice. Simon and Darius nodded in agreement. It took Rodelle a couple of seconds to remember that Jasmine had moved to the settlement's west side after her family home had all but collapsed around her while Rodelle was on the northern expedition.

"The seaside near the power plant is nicer," said Ollie, surprising everyone. "The beach is better than the west side. The west one is all rocks and stones."

"It is, but it's too close to the plant for it to be safe," Hannah replied. "There is equipment underwater that could be hazardous to a colony."

Speaking for the first time, the robed Si'laar said, "It

would not be peaceful while we rested." Their voice was crackly, like they were talking through the interstellar speaker in the comms tower. Maybe some kind of translation device Rodelle was unfamiliar with? Not that she knew of many, other than the one Jasmine had described to her from when she'd cruised through space to a waystation with her boyfriends, and that one had been hooked in her ear.

"The west side it is," said Hannah. "Korjek has told us that their crew intends to start construction tonight. Oh, this is Korjek." She gestured to the robed Si'laar. "This is Tibbot." Her voice took on a guttural growl as she tried to pronounce Tibbot's name, emphasizing the "T" sounds. Tibbot, the Si'laar wearing the shipsuit, looked amused at Hannah's attempt, their thin lips lifting in a smile that revealed their small, pointed white teeth.

"It is merely a matter of moving our pods from our starship to the water," Korjek explained.

At the mention of their ship, Hannah colored. "That brings us to another reason for this meeting. The cyborgs appear to have stolen the Si'laar's ship and tech a couple centuries ago."

"The Si'laar cloning technology was adapted for their use," Tibbot said, speaking for the first time. Their voice was heavily accented, a slightly lower pitch than Korjek's, but still retained the same soft, peaceful cadence. It also lacked the telltale crackle of a translation device, which meant they were speaking Standard, at least the dialect that was spoken on New Eden. Rodelle wondered how they were doing that. Could they really learn a language in a matter of hours?

"Our previous iterations stole it decades ago," explained Rhys. "We are not sure of the exact circumstances, but we have theorized that it was a calculated theft."

"Our records have all but been erased from the galaxy as we kept being displaced," added Korjek.

"What likely happened is, our previous iterations needed a more efficient method of cloning, found a peaceful race that was known for being unarmed, and took it." Rhys looked a little green as he reiterated the theory.

"There is no record of bloodshed in our oral tradition," Korjek said, as if to reassure Rhys. "An incident of that magnitude would have been passed down. When I examined your ship, I found traces of . . ." They paused, as if considering how their words could be translated. "Much of the data was missing, but there are traces of code that originated with the Si'laar. I recognized one of the codes as being from a . . . you might call it a yard. A shipyard, perhaps?"

Beside her, Brandon visibly relaxed. "Oh, thank God," he muttered.

Rodelle waited for Korjek to continue. "The ship may have been in a repair facility. Perhaps it was newly built. It was not taken in battle as the spoils of war."

A collective sigh of relief rippled through the crowd. Rhys's shoulders slumped, as if a physical load had just been lifted off his back.

"Also, the original settlers were part of an organized criminal enterprise and ran away to establish a colony here to get away from people they ripped off," announced Hannah.

The relieved murmurs gave way to a barrage of questions, shouted simultaneously. "Sorry," said Hannah over the crowd, holding up her hands in defeat. "I didn't think there was any reason to beat around the bush. We'd all started to suspect it, anyway. Evidence of that was found on the clearscreens Rodelle, Brandon, and CW44 brought back from the north."

"There is also the matter of the business conducted between our previous iterations and New Eden," said Rhys.

"They also brought James Thierry back from the north," added Hannah. The questions came faster, louder. Hannah's gaze caught Rodelle's, and she held up her hands again before letting them flop against her sides. She had completely lost control of the situation.

On the stage, Tibbot and Korjek exchanged an unreadable look. Rodelle wondered if they were reconsidering their choice to settle on New Eden. She wouldn't blame them if they did. Their first impressions had certainly been disastrous.

Over the din, Hannah said tiredly, "Why don't we just talk over each other until everyone has an idea of what's going on? We have a hospital now, too, before I forget to tell you." She sat down on the stage again as a group of New Edeners clustered around her, peppering her with questions. James stood and joined them, a temporary distraction as people greeted him, amazed that he was still alive.

Rodelle rose and Brandon followed suit. "I should help talk to them," she announced. "At least I can tell them what happened in the north."

"Everything?" Brandon asked, his voice a suggestive whisper in her ear. Her skin prickled with awareness, and for half a second, she wished they were back at home, away from the prying eyes of their fellow New Edeners.

Her face heated, and she knew a furious blush had to be creeping up her cheeks. "Of course not."

"I will, too, in that case. I *did* help to decode the

clearscreens." Squeezing her hand, he led her to the crowd. Into her hair, he murmured, "I think I love you."

She froze, looking up in shock. She hadn't expected that, not in a million years. "What?"

"I think I love you," he repeated. "I've never told that to anyone, and I've never experienced it. You don't have to say anything. I just wanted you to know."

It was a hell of a time to make that kind of declaration, but she wouldn't reject it. "How do you know?"

"I just do." Dimly, she was aware of Hannah trying to answer questions, but she sounded far away, as if Rodelle's brain had muted her. "I love everything about you."

Rodelle desperately wanted to tell him that she felt the same, that she was falling in love for the first time, but couldn't bring herself to. Brandon might very well walk back that statement when she told him about her role in Jackson's death. The darkest secret she had. One that she had sworn never to reveal. The secret that had kept her out of her own house for years, had kept her cut off from her friends from guilt.

She took a deep breath and kissed him, unable to speak about her feelings yet. It would have to do for now.

CHAPTER THIRTEEN

AN OVERWHELMING SENSE that he'd fucked up gnawed at Brandon. Should he have waited to lay out his feelings, maybe until his and Rodelle's relationship wasn't so fresh in its shift to physical? Maybe he shouldn't have said, *"I think I love you,"* because it was a lie, a way to insulate his heart against pain if she pushed him away. He didn't think he loved her—he knew he did. He didn't have to experience love before to know what he was feeling now. Did she not like the part where he'd said, "I think"?

After the meeting at the amphitheater, he and Rodelle ambled home, fingers laced together as they walked. She was still amenable to touching him—in fact, her grip felt tighter than usual, as if she was afraid he would stride away from her. But she had a worried, pinched look on her face that he wished he could smooth away, and her replies to his observations about the Si'laar and the meeting were abrupt, single word answers. It was like every bit of excitement she'd had about New Eden's latest arrivals had evaporated.

He waited until they were home and the door closed behind him before he said, "Tell me what I did wrong."

She looked surprised at the question. "You didn't do anything wrong."

"Did I speak too soon at the amphitheater? I meant every word." Remembering how he's said, *"I think,"* he quickly added, "Well, sort of." Her eyes widened in surprise and hurt. "I don't think I love you. I know I do."

Color rose to her cheeks and the tips of her ears. His cybernetics reported to him that her heart rate had increased and body temperature slightly rose. He squeezed her hand, hoping it was a reassuring gesture. "I'm glad," she said softly.

"Does it bother you?"

Rodelle withdrew her hand and looked away. Now it was his turn to feel hurt, an unfamiliar pain that lanced his enhanced heart. "Not in the way you think," she said hurriedly, noticing his mood shift. "What if I told you I didn't deserve it?"

That statement took him aback. "What? Of course you do. Is this about your husband?" He hated having to bring him up but couldn't think of any other reason she would say something so awful.

A muscle ticked in her jaw, and he knew he was right. "What did he tell you?" he pressed. He kept his voice level, gentle, not wanting to alarm her. "What kind of bullshit was he filling your head with?"

Rodelle still flinched at the question. "Do I have to talk about it now?"

"You don't have to do anything you don't want to. I just want to know that you—that *we're*—a team. That we're still good," he emphasized. "There's nothing you could do that would not make me love you."

Tears filled her eyes. She took a step back, covering her

mouth with her hand. He didn't move, not wanting to scare her. "I'm not sure that's true."

"Rodelle, what could you have possibly done?"

She swiped away her tears with the back of her hand. "It was bad." She barked out a harsh, humorless half-laugh, muffled by a sob. "I don't want to tell you, but I can't have you thinking that you love me if I don't tell you what I did. I feel like a fucking fraud."

"You've been through a lot of stress the last couple of years, and we got back from a major exploration this morning, during which we found one of your friends you'd written off as dead. I think you're being really hard on yourself." Brandon's mind whirled, trying to figure out a way to make this situation better, make Rodelle feel better, to help her see herself as he saw her.

"It was stressful before the earthquake. That just changed the kind of stress I had to live with." She looked around the kitchen with a critical eye. "I think I want to tear down this house and build a new one."

"That's a solid plan, and I'd love to help you with that. Just—just talk to me," he pleaded. "I meant what I said. We're a team."

"Okay."

"Okay, what?"

"Okay, I'll talk to you." She pulled out one of the wooden chairs from the table and plunked into it. Despite her small size, the wood creaked ominously under her weight, a reminder of the furniture's age. "Sit." He did so, pulling a chair and moving it so he could sit next to her. Instead, she rose. "I think I'll need a drink for this." Opening a cupboard, she removed a glass bottle of dandelion wine, the only libation available on New Eden. "Want some?"

His cybernetics would filter out the wine's alcohol

content, leaving him only with the beverage's terrible taste to pretend to enjoy. Still, he nodded. "I'll have some if you are."

Woodenly, Rodelle poured a generous amount into a pair of earthenware mugs and brought them to the table. She took a healthy swallow of it and looked in the mug before speaking. "I told you Jackson and I didn't have a good marriage."

"You did."

"Both of our families were big deals once upon a time, with his family, the Lansings, being one of the first groups to settle here. Mine were the Redfields. I guess great-great-however many great grandpa Lansing was a criminal, now that we know what we do about New Eden. Our parents set us up to be married when we were young, like fourteen or fifteen."

"You were married off when you were fourteen?" Outrage colored Brandon's words, and his hand involuntarily clenched into a fist. If Rodelle's parents were here, he would have them knocked out on the cracked tile floor.

"No, I was twenty when we got married. It was arranged when we were younger. Both of our parents wanted to see at least one couple live out their lives, and we were the right ages." She shrugged and looked away. "There weren't a lot of people to choose from, as you know by now. There were fewer than ten young people, teenagers, when I was growing up, and Jackson and I weren't related. It was important to our families that we marry and start a family. I think James was supposed to marry a girl called Jennifer, but she died from a fever when she was seven or eight years old, and . . ." She sighed. "I'm babbling." She took another swallow of wine.

"Was that common, arranged marriages?" he prompted.

"Not until relatively recently. The original settlement had over a hundred people, and they had babies, a lot of them at first. As long as people weren't related—no closer than third cousins, at least—you could marry anyone you wanted." She looked at him over the rim of her mug. "James and Ollie West are distant cousins, I think. Jasmine is related to him a few generations back too."

Brandon didn't want to talk about James or Jasmine, but stayed silent, waiting for her to tell her story on her terms.

"Jackson and I got married," she continued. "He was always pretty entitled, pretty full of himself because he was one of the only boys in New Eden. The only other one in our generation who made it to adulthood is James. Jackson made it clear he could've had any other woman he wanted." A shudder rippled through her. "The woman closest in age to me is Hannah. I'm six years older than her. I used to babysit her, for God's sake. That bastard wouldn't have seen anything wrong with marrying a four-teen-year-old."

Not for the first time, Brandon wished that Jackson was alive, just so he could personally kill him. "That's disgusting. No one called him out on that?"

"I'm the only person who he said that to. Please don't tell Hannah," she pleaded. "Don't tell anyone. Not because I don't want people to think badly of him, but—" Her eyes filled with tears again. "We've been through enough."

"Of course I won't." He ached to touch her, to wrap her small hands in his in an attempt to comfort her, but refrained from doing so. She was opening up, talking to him the way he'd wished she would.

"He was always so mean to me." Her voice came out in a pained whisper. "He made a big show of being New Eden's leader, calling himself a mayor, like this was a real city. Jackson was polite to other people to get them to do what he wanted. He was a good manipulator."

"How so?"

"He got half the settlement to build our stupid little guesthouse shed thing in the yard for him," she replied. "He didn't cut down the lumber himself; he had others do it. He stood back and let everyone else construct it while telling them what to do. When repairs had to be made to this place, he took supplies from other houses. He literally helped himself to floor tiles to replace ones in here that broke or wore out. He was always the first to take a bottle of wine when other people made it, the first to help himself to food. Just selfish shit, you know?

"But, at first, there were times he was kind to me, and for the first couple of years we lived together, things weren't horrible. I didn't love him, exactly, and I'm not sure he loved me, either. After about three years, he really started being awful in private—nitpicking everything I did and said. He would get pissed off that I spent time with Hannah and Jasmine and said I should be at home instead."

"Trying to isolate you?" Brandon asked.

"Moreso than we already were. I didn't listen to him and kept up my friendships with them. They were all I had after my parents died when I was in my early twenties. Dad probably died from food poisoning complications after he ate some undercooked food. A few other people got sick, too, but he was the only person who died. My mother— I'm not sure. She just didn't wake up one morning," Rodelle explained. The pain in her voice pulled at Brandon. "It was like her heart just stopped. Maybe it did, I don't know." She paused to dab at her eyes with the hem of her shirt. Her eyes met his. "I can't believe I'm telling you this."

He shook his head. "You didn't do anything wrong."

"I'm not done yet. Jackson got worse after a few years together—throwing things in my direction, then throwing things at me. He talked about having a baby, which I thought was insane, even though that was the whole point of our getting married. He got angry when I didn't get pregnant, and I know now that I probably couldn't from nutritional deficiencies, and yet . . ." She sniffled. "In another life, I would've loved to have had kids. I really wanted them, actually, but not on New Eden and not with Jackson. I gave up on the idea of children a long time ago."

Part of Brandon wanted to reassure her that she could have them if she wanted, that he would have liked to have them with her, but stayed silent. Some other time, maybe.

"He started hitting me about a year before the quake," she said. Her voice rose in pitch, like she'd had to force herself to say the words. "Just a . . . a slap once in a while, not too hard, then it got more frequent. He killed my pet hen, too. He . . ."

"What the fuck?" Brandon couldn't keep the outrage out of his voice. She flinched, a faraway look in her eyes as she relived what had happened to her.

"I raised Gracie from a chick. I took her from the agri-center about six years ago, maybe? She was supposed to be food, but I decided to keep her as a pet. I'd never had one before, and I'd always wanted a companion animal. She was so sweet. She would follow me around the yard and sit with me sometimes, when I was reading or sewing." She swallowed, now weeping openly. Brandon's stomach lurched as he waited for her next words, knowing they were going to be awful.

"He killed her one afternoon," she whispered. Her eyes had taken on a faraway look as she remembered what must have been a horrible day. "I wasn't there, thank God. I was visiting with Hannah and Jasmine. I was trying to avoid Jackson. He'd started getting really mean around then, and he took it out on Gracie. I came home, and he said she just fell over and died, but he was smirking when he said it, like he was trying to look sad and . . ." Her voice trailed off. "I knew. He wanted to *eat* her, the fucking bastard. He wrung her neck himself."

Brandon felt his own eyes prickle with unshed tears of grief and rage on her behalf. She had shrunk in on herself as she spoke, wrapping her arms around her midsection, her gaze glassy and focused on something behind him that only she could see. He had no words to console her, no idea how to help her. So, he waited for her to continue when she was ready.

His internal chronometer told him a full two minutes passed before she spoke again. "I didn't let him eat Gracie. I insisted on burying her in the cemetery. I would've liked to do that in the backyard, but he would've gotten angry all over again whenever he saw the little headstone I made. It wasn't worth the fights."

"What he did to you wasn't fighting," Brandon said. "That implies that there was a measure of equality between you two."

Rodelle gave him the barest of nods. She blinked, as if to clear her vision, like Brandon speaking reminded her that he was here and she was safe. "I guess so. The quake happened a few months after Gracie died," she continued. Looking away again, she wiped her eyes with the hem of her tunic. "He'd been getting worse at home and starting to leave bruises in places I couldn't easily hide.

"There was a community meeting the night of the quake." Her voice dropped to nearly a whisper again as she remembered. "He left early, and he was already pissed off because one of the few people left who knew how to make major repairs at the power station had passed away a couple of weeks before. Michael Davis, his name was. He'd been trying to write manuals for the power station as best he could, but there were so few replacement components available in New Eden, and he had to improvise with what he had. He said he had arthritis, too, which just made Jackson angrier."

"How did Michael die?" Brandon asked, fearing the answer.

"He passed in his sleep. Natural causes. Jackson didn't kill him." Rodelle took a deep breath, clearly steeling herself. "He left early the night of the quake. I didn't want to go. I—my eye was bruised. I didn't want anyone to see."

Brandon's hand involuntarily clenched into a fist. Part of him wanted to dig up Jackson, take some of his DNA, and clone him, just so Brandon could kill him again with his bare hands.

Rodelle's eyes glazed over again. "The ground shook. I was here, in the kitchen, when it started, and I thought the world was going to split apart and swallow us whole. It happened so fast, I remember it feeling loud. Can things *feel* loud?" She didn't seem to expect an answer. Brandon wasn't sure she remembered he was there at that moment.

"When it stopped, I ran outside. Some of the houses had just collapsed, like they were made of twigs. Some of them probably were. And I could see the old community center from here, and it was gone. Fallen in on itself. I heard people screaming, and I remember Hannah was beside herself. Her parents were inside when the roof collapsed, and she was pushing away stones and bricks to get to them, even though she knew . . ." Rodelle paused.

"I looked for Jackson. I found him trapped under a section of roof that had broken off, and he was still alive. His legs were crushed, I think. I didn't look too closely. He couldn't get up, and his face was covered in blood. When he tried to speak, he coughed up more of it." Rodelle looked down at her hands, now knotted together in her lap. "I nudged the piece of roof and brick pillar just enough so it fell on his head. It killed him right away. *I* killed him."

Brandon had a notion that Rodelle's story was leaning in that direction, but he was still unprepared for the impact of her whispered words. She had been in an untenable situation, one that would have ultimately ended up with her being murdered at her husband's hand, had the earthquake not happened.

Her shoulders heaved in a fresh sob. "I didn't have a choice. And I had a crazy thought that my life might get better with Jackson dead, but then it hit me that we now had to live with only a few survivors after it, and of course, it didn't get better. It was just a different kind of worse." She looked up, raising a tear-stained face to look at Brandon. "I couldn't get out of bed for years. I felt guilty about not feeling guilty for killing my husband. How fucked up is that? Once I helped with the cleanup and burying people, I couldn't do anything else but lie in bed and wait for my turn to die." With that announcement, she burst into tears.

"Rodelle." Brandon made sure his voice was as calm and soothing as he could make it.

She didn't stop crying, but her swollen eyes met his.

"I'm not upset. I don't think any less of you. I also don't think you killed Jackson, but I don't blame you for doing what you did."

She sniffled. "You don't?"

"No. If he was coughing blood, his ribs likely punctured his lungs, and he was going to die, anyway. But even if he could have been saved, no one in the civilized universe would find fault for you killing him." He reached for her hands, unsure how he would be received during such a vulnerable moment. They shook under his touch, the tremors coursing through them so fine and minute that he wouldn't have been able to sense them had his skin not been enhanced.

A few seconds later, she closed the distance between them, crawling into his lap. Face buried in his shoulder, she wordlessly sobbed, gripping him like he was a lifeline. Brandon wrapped his arms around her, hoping it would provide a measure of comfort to her, however small it may be.

Moments ticked by that Brandon didn't bother to count. Rodelle raised her head. "I've never told anyone that."

"It's your story to tell on your terms." He stroked her hair, hoping he was providing at least a small measure of comfort.

She lowered her head to his shoulder again. "I only just told Hannah and Jasmine how awful things were between us a few weeks ago. I don't know how to tell them I killed Jackson, even if you think I didn't."

"You don't have to tell them anything you don't want to. I don't think they would judge you for it, but you know them better than I do." He pressed a kiss to the top of her head. The smell of her soap and skin was a comfort to him, as was the warm weight of her against his chest. "You have my word that I will never tell anyone about this."

"You don't hate me?"

"I could never hate you." Quite the opposite, in fact.

"Thank you."

Brandon couldn't tell if Rodelle was thanking him for listening, or for staying with her after her confession, and didn't ask. She needed support, and he was only too happy to provide it. She snuggled against him, her breath evening out as she finally relaxed for the first time in years.

CHAPTER FOURTEEN

Rodelle was unsure how much time had passed while she let Brandon hold her. The relief that poured through her after telling him about her role in Jackson's death was immeasurable, which she hadn't expected. The guilt that had tainted her conscience for years was finally fading a little, even though the logical part of her brain had always told her that she shouldn't feel guilty for killing a man who would have eventually taken her life if he'd survived the quake.

Head leaning against his chest, she listened to the steady beat of his enhanced heart, the gentle thumps almost hypnotic. In another scenario, she could fall asleep in this position. She shifted, prompting Brandon to tighten his hold on her. "Thank you," she murmured.

"What for?"

"For listening. For seeing things from my perspective. I don't know anyone else who was abused by their spouse. It must have happened at some point, but no one talked about it."

"He would have killed you someday," he replied, echoing her earlier thoughts.

"I know that now. Maybe he would have made it look like an accident." A horrific notion struck her. "That must've been—oh, my God. I wonder how many accidents over the years were really deliberate. How many people really murdered their spouses and pretended they'd just fallen out of a tree or drowned?" A fresh wave of tears filled her eyes as a newfound rage took hold of her. "Is it like this in the rest of the universe?"

"Possibly. There are serious consequences for abusers elsewhere in the galaxy, if it does. And you have my word that nothing like that will ever happen again as long as I— as long as the rest of the cyborgs—live here."

Slightly mollified, Rodelle nodded against his chest. "Thank you."

A few moments passed before she spoke again. "I'm glad you're here with me now, but I don't think I want to stay in this house. I don't know if we can ever make enough good memories to wash away the bad."

"Hey, if you want to knock this place down and rebuild something that will hold up better in an earthquake, I'm all for it."

Rodelle refrained from pointing out that the house was already pretty solid, having survived the quake in the first place with little damage, aside from some loose bricks. "Do you think there will be enough pre-fab houses to go around?"

"I think there will be more than enough after the next couple of supply runs, considering New Eden wants other people to eventually move here. And I'm not an engineer, by any means, but I do know that all of the existing housing stock will eventually have to be replaced just due to age."

"We'll build a house with your dream kitchen."

"I like the sound of that. I've never had one."

"Your original did," she pointed out.

"I'm pretty sure my original only worked in the kitchens of his dreams and couldn't afford to actually own a home that would have one. He was probably pretty poor, if he signed up for the original cyborg project."

"How often do you think of him?"

He shrugged. "Not that much. I'm not him, I don't want to be him, and he must have had other choices to earn money than joining a black ops military operation when he didn't have any experience. I wish I had his body art, though. I do remember that."

Rodelle was intrigued. "What kind of body art?"

"Brayden Emerson had tattoos. Both arms full of them."

"Like, ink was injected into the skin? I've read about them, but I've never seen one."

"Yes, Brayden was quite the tattoo enthusiast. I don't remember what the designs looked like, exactly, just that some of them were of trees and bushes maybe, and that he was proud of them. I think they were expensive, which might account for why he signed up for a military experiment. I don't know." She thought she could hear him smile as he spoke. "I wouldn't mind having that again, though I have no idea where to get tattoo supplies. I think my cybernetics would heal the skin, anyway."

"You have your hardware. I think you can count that as body art," she said, thinking of the metal components in his skin. She now knew where every piece was on his body.

"Mm, I do. Not quite the same thing, though."

Rodelle unfolded herself from his lap, the need to stretch her legs sudden and nearly overwhelming. Her face felt puffy and tight from crying, but otherwise, she felt, well, not *good*, exactly, but better. Almost refreshed now that she had the weight of Jackson's death off her conscience. "Thank you," she said.

He hadn't moved from his seat. "For what?"

"Just everything. For listening to me and not pretending that everything is okay, but that my feelings are important. I'm not over everything that's happened, but I feel like I made a start to being there tonight. Thank you."

Brandon rose, gathering her in his arms again. She leaned into him, inhaling his scent of clean skin and soap. "This is what couples do. We're supposed to listen to each other."

"You've been a part of a couple before?" she teased.

"No, but I'm familiar with the concept. And I'm going to be the best partner to you that I can be. I meant it when I said I love you, Rodelle."

She froze, hardly daring to believe her ears. She didn't know if she would ever get used to hearing those words. Her face was wet again as tears trickled down her cheeks. "I love you too. I'm glad we can stumble around this together."

"Always. I'm not going anywhere."

———

SUNLIGHT FILTERED through the thin curtains in the bedroom, the first morning Brandon woke next to Rodelle in bed. After weeks of sleeping on the ramshackle couch, with Rodelle in the backyard shed—so close and yet so far away—it was wonderful to have everything he'd wanted since the cyborg ship landed on New Eden.

She was curled up on her side next to him, a few strands of dark blonde hair falling over her eyes. Taking care not to disturb her, he shifted so he could see her better. She was naked under the sheets, as was he. Neither of them had felt particularly sexy after her confession last night, even though he'd made one of his own, but they'd needed the physical contact when they finally crawled into bed in a tangle of limbs.

Rodelle stirred, eyes blinking. "Good morning." The greeting was punctuated by a yawn. She brushed her hair out of her eyes and levered up on one elbow to better look at him.

"How are you feeling this morning?"

"Like a million-kilo weight has been lifted off me. I actually feel . . ." A pensive look crossed her expression. "A new kind of optimistic. I started feeling better about New Eden when you showed up, but now I feel like I have a future of my own. Like I can finally move forward."

He traced the back of his hand down her face, noting with pride how the small gesture teased a gasp from her. Her pupils dilated, something he might not have noticed had his vision not been enhanced as it was. He bit back a knowing grin, wanting everything that could happen next to be on her terms.

Rodelle leaned in, closing the small distance between them with a kiss. Brandon's body immediately responded, and he eagerly returned it, his hand reaching for her bare hip under the sheet. She shifted, bringing herself closer to him until their skin met. Her nipples scraped across his chest, the heat of her lower body feeling as hot as an inferno where it touched his belly. A shudder of pleasure rippled through him, and his cock immediately strained against her.

She pulled him on top of her, kissing him with an urgency that left him breathless. He was only too happy to oblige. Her leg wrapped around his hip, pulling him to her, her own hips lifting a little to meet his body, as if she couldn't wait to have him inside her. Brandon pressed a kiss to her neck, where her pulse fluttered wildly against his lips. A breathy moan escaped Rodelle's throat, and he quickly shifted positions to take her lips again.

Rodelle reached between their bodies, wrapping her hand around his erection that was already aching. Wordlessly, she guided him into her warm, wet heat, both of them breathing a sigh of relief and pleasure when he was fully seated inside her. He withdrew and thrust into her again, drawing a small cry from Rodelle, the sound enough to cease all of his rational thought.

"Do it," she murmured in his ear. "You won't hurt me."

That was all the encouragement he needed. He pounded into her, vaulting himself up on his elbows enough so he could see her face, how her eyes were glazed with lust, her full lips swollen from his kisses. Her hands held tight against his back, nails digging into his skin so hard they might leave marks. The tiny pinpricks of pain only bolstered him, as did her breathy moans. Beneath him, her body stiffened a little before her inner walls started to contract. She was on the verge of an orgasm, one he was only too happy to give her.

She cried out when her climax hit, biting into his shoulder to muffle the noise. Brandon's muscles tightened, and he knew he wasn't far behind. *Goddamn it, I wanted to last a little longer.*

He couldn't bring himself to feel any regret as he came hard and fast, a growl leaving him as he rutted into her like an animal. He couldn't find his voice until he finished, then reluctantly pulled out of her and gathered her in his arms. When he did, all he could say was, "Fuck."

Rodelle's voice still sounded out of breath. "I can't believe that."

"What? Why not? That was great!" He tightened his arm holding her in place against his chest.

Her soft giggle reverberated through his body. "It's never been like that before. I've never been like that before. I needed it."

"I think I did too." He draped the sheet over them when he saw her shiver a little. Brandon could feel his own sweat evaporating off his skin. His sensors automatically adjusted themselves to slightly raise his temperature to compensate.

She raised her head, an unexpectedly serious look on her face. "I love you."

A thrill coursed through him at the words, ones he would never tire of. "I love you too."

Any further conversation was halted by the sound of a knock at the front door. "What the hell?" Rodelle murmured, sitting up.

"I'll get it."

"We could ignore it," she said hopefully.

"Good point." Brandon relaxed again, and Rodelle lay back against the pillows. They were thinner than he'd like —they could hardly be expected to sufficiently support her in slumber. Brandon had quickly adapted to regular humanoid sleeping habits, too, and would never willingly sleep in a recharging pod again if he didn't have to. They needed new pillows, immediately.

He remembered that they were sleeping and fucking in a broken bed. A new bed was definitely on the list too. It would be the first thing they'd get after the house was knocked down and a new pre-fab home constructed with the kitchen of his dreams.

"You're smiling," Rodelle said. "What are you thinking about?"

"That I'm really looking forward to starting a new life with you."

A becoming blush touched her cheeks. "Me too."

Behind the curtains, someone tapped at the window. "Rodelle? Brandon?" It sounded like James.

"What's he doing here?" Rodelle climbed out of bed and grabbed a threadbare tunic lying on the floor. Padding to the window, she pushed the curtains out of the way and cranked it open. "James? What's going on? Is everything all right?"

At least the window was high enough that James wouldn't be able to see her lower half. Brandon had never thought of himself as the jealous type, but he apparently was.

"Why didn't you come to the door?" James asked.

"Because I was sleeping!"

"Oh." It sounded like James hadn't considered the possibility of people still resting in the morning. "Oh, sorry about that. Wanna check out the agri-center? They made a mistake when they cloned some animals, and we're allowed to take them as pets!" He sounded delighted, not sorry in the least.

From his spot on the bed, Brandon's ears perked up. "What do you mean, cloning mistake?"

"Is Brandon there? Hey! Yeah, so, I don't know how it happened, exactly, considering I didn't know clones existed until a few days ago, but there was a mistake. Connor's swearing a lot about it, and the long and short of it is, I think I'm getting a pet. Do you want one? They're pretty cute."

Brandon thought about Rodelle's pet hen, and his heart squeezed. "Rodelle," he said, hoping the discussion of companion animals wouldn't be painful.

"I'll be there soon," she said, surprising him. "Give me

a few minutes to wash up and get dressed."

———

A FEW PEOPLE milled around the barn when Rodelle arrived, Brandon at her side. Once her irritation at James's appearance at her bedroom window dissipated, she'd been intrigued by his announcement of a cloning mistake. "Should I be more worried?" she asked him. "No one seems to be upset about whatever happened."

"It's only nine in the morning. There's plenty of time for people to be upset."

As they got closer to the barn, Rodelle realized that some people were cradling little furry bundles in their hands. They must be the pets. Excitement welled in her. What were the animals?

Spotting Jasmine, she quickly walked to her, noting her friend looked like she had just rolled out of bed. Her blonde hair stuck up at all angles. She held a bundle in her arms, too, which raised a small gray head with triangular ears, tufts of white fur sprouting from them. It opened its mouth and let out a squeak. "Rodelle!" said Jasmine excitedly. "They made kittens accidentally!"

Rodelle halted, Jasmine's words taking a few seconds to sink in. "Like baby cats? The cyborgs accidentally made *baby cats?*"

"Yes! I guess they bought a barn in a box pre-fab thing at the waystation, which included feline DNA? Anyway, New Eden now has cats!" Jasmine stroked her finger over the tiny creature's head, who mewled again.

"Oh, my God!" Rodellle reached out to touch the kitten, surprised how soft its ears felt. It raised a paw and swatted at her with tiny claws that were sharper than she was expecting. "Ow."

"Yeah, he's a firecracker." Jasmine cuddled the kitten to her chest. "I have to talk to Darius and Simon about what we should name him. I should also tell them we now have a kitten. They got up early today to help with the new pre-fab house construction."

Rodelle looked back at Brandon, who was still staring at the kitten, agog. "Let's get one."

"I've never had a cat before," he said.

"Neither have I. It'll be fun, having a pet!"

"They poop in boxes," said Jasmine helpfully.

"Ugh." Despite his reaction, Brandon didn't look dissuaded hearing that bit of news. "Are there any kitten clones left? It looks like everyone here has one."

"I think there's ten or eleven altogether, so a couple are left." The kitten in Jasmine's arms mewled again and climbed up her tunic. "Ow, his nails are sharp. Easy!" She settled the animal against her shoulder like a baby.

A wave of longing swept through Rodelle. She'd never seen a cat before; no one on New Eden had, only having read about them in books. Without another word, she took off through the open barn door.

CW44—*Connor*, she corrected herself—wore a look of aggravation as his gaze swept over a high-sided pen. From inside, squeaks and meows sounded. Seeing Rodelle, Connor said, "They were supposed to be goat embryos. You can imagine my surprise this morning when I checked the livestock cloning tanks to see *this*." He waved a dismissive hand over the pen.

Rodelle looked over at the trio of kittens inside, crawling over each other. "They're adorable!" She reached over, petting a couple of furry heads.

"They are unnecessary on a planet without vermin, and an invasive species where the chicken population is concerned," Connor replied.

"How are they a threat to the chickens? They're so small!" A long-whiskered, black-and-white cat sniffed Rodelle's hand, then rubbed its head against her with a squeaky trill. Her heart felt like it might melt in on itself. Taking care, she gently picked up the kitten, who meowed again.

"They will grow up and be a menace," Connor vowed.

James entered the barn, holding a pair of orange kittens in his arms. "These little guys are mine," he announced.

"How will you tell them apart?" Rodelle asked.

"Oh, this little guy on my right is Rusty. He meows a lot more and it sounds rusty." James laughed at his own joke. "The one on my left is Charlie. I just liked the sound of the name."

"They meow the exact same amount. They're two of the same cat. They're cloned from the same DNA," Connor replied.

"Yeah, they're twin brothers. I didn't want to split up twin brothers."

"They're not . . ." Connor's lips thinned. "Fine, they're twins."

"I can see their whiskers are a little different on the right sides of their noses, like by an eighth of a centimeter. That's how I can tell them apart."

"How can you see that?" Brandon asked suspiciously.

"I have a new cyborg eye, my friend. Remember? Connor gave me a new eye, and I gave him a name."

"You wouldn't stop pestering me until I agreed to acknowledge a so-called regular name in the future," Connor said irritably. Rodelle fought back a smile. The kitten mewled in her hands, then head-butted her chest. She stroked the side of its neck, surprised when it vibrated under her fingers.

"She's purring," Connor said, nodding his head at the kitten.

"She's a girl?" Rodelle asked.

"There were eleven kittens mistakenly produced. Six males, five females. I do wonder how Hannah will react to this news. She does not strike me as someone who wants to see an invasive species take hold on New Eden. They will have to be desexed."

"No one's told Hannah yet?" Rodelle asked in surprise.

"Nah, she didn't answer the door when I knocked." One of James's kittens meowed, a long wail. "Rusty, it's all good. You're gonna like our new house. It'll be finished soon, so we can get used to it together. I stayed with Ollie last night, and I don't know if he'd want cats around. We're going to have a great time, I promise." His hair nearly matched his kittens' fur.

The sight of her old friend speaking so tenderly to his new pets brought tears to Rodelle's eyes. When she looked down at the black-and-white kitten of her own, they fell, a few drops landing on her fur. She sniffled, louder than she would have liked. "Sorry," she said when she caught Connor's quizzical look. Brandon wrapped an arm around her and pressed a reassuring kiss to her temple. To Connor, she said, "Thank you."

"You're thanking me for an accident?"

"A very happy accident," she clarified. She shifted the kitten in her arms, so she could wipe away her tears. "She's so cute. I'm going to give her such a good home." She gazed down at the little creature, who returned her stare with big golden eyes. Her whiskers quivered.

"Why is everyone—" Hannah's voice was outside the barn. "What the hell, Jasmine? Is that a *cat* you're holding?"

CHAPTER FIFTEEN

THE SUNS WERE SETTING when the Si'laar roused themselves. Brandon recognized Tibbot, the only one who wore a shipsuit, all four of their arms waving hello in a very human-like greeting as he and Rodelle took an evening walk around the settlement. "Good evening." Their brow furrowed when they saw the kitten in Rodelle's arms.

"Did you have a good sleep?"

"My regeneration was productive, although I am looking ahead to spending the time underwater when our submersible pods are completed." Tibbot paused. "Is that the correct phrase? 'Looking ahead'? I installed a Standard language program before I regenerated."

"Looking ahead, looking forward, both work," said Rodelle.

"You can download language programs into your brain?" Brandon asked.

Tibbot tilted their head in a way that was almost human. "You cannot?"

"Well, we probably could, but we just never bothered to. Aural translators have always worked for us."

"Understood." Tibbot gestured to the kitten. "What is this fauna? Our ship did not detect animals other than the livestock from your ancestors' original planet."

"This is a kitten," said Rodelle, running a finger down the animal's nose. She meowed in response. Rodelle smiled in a way Brandon had never seen from her before, one of contentment. "She's a baby cat. There was a mix-up with some of the DNA brought here for cloning, and now New Eden has cats. We're keeping them as pets."

"A companion animal," Tibbot deduced. "May I touch it?"

Brandon recognized Korjek and nodded in greeting as they walked past, flanked by a few other Si'laar still wearing their voluminous robes. The Si'laar looked at the kitten with what he guessed was curiosity but didn't stop their strolling.

Rodelle held out the kitten. "Of course. I haven't picked a name for her yet."

Tibbot stroked a long, pale finger down the kitten's back. She stretched, trying to get closer to them. "Do you want to hold her?" Rodelle asked.

"I do not know how. Perhaps when she is not so small." The kitten mewled before nuzzling her head into Rodelle's chest. Ahead of them, Korjek turned around and gazed at Tibbot, expression unreadable. Tibbot nodded in response. "Korjek is convening with your leaders. My presence is requested." They sounded exasperated, like a kid being told to hurry up by a parent. "I am certain we will speak later." With a wave of their right hands, they took off with surprising speed to where the rest of the Si'laar were waiting.

"It's going to be wild sorting out the social aspect of

their living here," said Rodelle as they retreated. "Tibbot seems to be keen on making friends. Their Standard is great."

"The ability to learn a whole new language while sleeping would be convenient," Brandon agreed. The kitten meowed and reached out a paw toward Brandon. "Can I take her?"

"Of course." Rodelle gently handed her over to him. "You could develop a cat language translator. The first collaborative project between New Eden, the cyborgs, and the Si'laar." She grinned, eyes sparkling.

"That sounds ambitious."

"Rebuilding New Eden is ambitious," she pointed out. She stroked the kitten's face, who leaned into her. "Have you thought about names?"

"I was going to leave that to you."

"I have too many ideas right now. I haven't named anything since . . ." Her expression shuttered for a few seconds. Brandon knew she was thinking about Gracie, her murdered pet hen. "Well, you know. I like Honey, Angel, Joy, and Cassie. The last two were my mother's and aunt's names. It's probably weird to name a cat after your mom, so it's between Honey and Angel. I think they're cute for a cat."

"I like either."

"So do I. That's why it's so hard to choose. Also, I thought if I ever had daughters, I'd name them after my mom and aunt, so I should probably save those for later." As she said the words, a stricken look crossed her face, as if she couldn't believe they had left her mouth.

Brandon spotted Rhys and Hannah heading to the agri-center, the same direction the Si'laar had headed. They both waved, and out of politeness, Brandon waved in response before turning back to Rodelle. "It's fine if you want to have children. You've already said as much. I'd like to be a dad one day." He'd floated the idea a little since he and Rodelle had grown closer, and he liked it.

Something in her expression shifted, and her eyes filled with tears. "Thank you."

"For what? I mean, you're welcome, but I'm not sure what you're thanking me for. It's okay to want to have a family. You're finally in a place where that could be feasible."

"What if I can't have children? I couldn't before," she said quietly. Her voice was tinged with sadness.

"It could have been your husband who was the reason for that," Brandon pointed out. "Maybe it was due to nutritional deficiencies or a medical condition, as you've suggested. Who knows? We'll have the ability to find that out very soon. Hell, maybe CW44 could do an exam for you tomorrow, now that the hospital's been built." He scanned the horizon, the hospital in view, a welcome sight on a planet without adequate healthcare for so many years. Its sides were blue, the inter-galactic standard color that marked it as a medical facility. "I have no idea what I'm doing with kids, though. We should probably read up on child development before we have our own. But, yes, I want them with you."

A few tears slid down her cheeks, which she hastily wiped away. She smiled. "That means a lot to me."

The kitten burrowed into his chest, its tiny claws lancing his skin through his shirt. "Damn. Not you, the cat. Her nails are sharper than you'd expect for something so small." Still, he cuddled her with one hand. With his free arm, he pulled Rodelle close to him. "I love you. I meant it when I said that. I'm looking forward to our life together, starting with building a new house."

"With the kitchen of your dreams."

"And room for children."

They paused outside a newly built pre-fab house, the sides so white they would dazzle in the sun. The front door opened and James stepped out. Spotting Rodelle and Brandon, he waved. "I like your cat! Mine are doing great!" he called. He bounded toward them on bare feet. At least he was wearing clothes, although Brandon was sure he was only doing so begrudgingly. "What are you two up to?"

"Just going for a walk. It's a nice night," Rodelle replied.

"You should see what the suns look like setting in the north. Just incredible." He sounded wistful as he said the words, giving Brandon the impression that he missed his old home. Just as quickly, James recovered. "But I wouldn't have my cats in the north, so it's a good trade-off, I guess."

"We did see the suns set," Rodelle pointed out.

"Only a couple of times, though, right? It's not the same. It's very peaceful to see them on the water. I bet it would be an even more spectacular sight if I saw them with my new eye." As if to emphasize his new organ, he blinked. Brandon's own enhanced vision could pick up his eye's details, the microscopic components hidden behind a blue iris. "Anyway, if I have to stay here, at least I have a pretty nice house that won't fall down if there's another earthquake. I didn't think this place could get any more depressing, and obviously I can see it's improving, but when you talk about the quake, everyone's faces just kind of shut down, you know? Like, no one wants to remember it, but they can't help it. I didn't feel anything in the caves when it happened, but I might have been asleep. I don't know."

Brandon caught Rodelle's eye as James babbled, unsure

how to respond. She looked like she had no idea how to react, either.

James continued. "I'm really glad I don't have to live with anyone right now. Connor said I would irritate any potential roommate into running to the north to escape my 'endless chatter,' as he puts it, but I think that's a bit harsh. Maybe they'd just go outside. I can take a hint, eventually. My cats don't mind my talking. Do you?" He tilted his head expectantly.

My God, has he taken a hint?

"No," replied Rodelle automatically. "I'm glad you're back and you missed the worst of the quake's effects. I *like* that you're upbeat about all of this. That's really hard to do."

"Well, I have to be upbeat," James said.

"No, you don't."

"I really do. It's just easier that way. Can I walk with you? I'll get my cats. I made them little leashes."

"Of course," replied Brandon.

"Great! I'll be right back." He dashed back to his house, emerging a few moments later with his pair of orange kittens. They now sported tiny harnesses and leads made from the thick flexiwire used to insulate cables on starships. "Aren't these great? Connor helped me find the material."

It was going to take a while for Brandon to think of CW44 as Connor. His fellow cyborg had always preferred their traditional ways—not choosing a name other than his numerical designation, continuing to wear his black ship-suit long after most of the others opted for the tunics and shorts popular among New Edeners, and communicating with other cyborgs via their shared link instead of speaking. Knowing James expected an answer, Brandon looked at the kittens and said, "Yes."

"Come on, boys," said James soothingly. "Let's walk." One of them meowed in response but took a few steps on tiny paws. The other plunked down on the grass. James crouched, picked up the kitten, so he was standing on all four legs, then pulled the leashes a little, urging them to move. They did, taking a few steps alongside him, the leads wrapping around each other. "Let's go to the hospital," he said, and Brandon suspected James was talking to the cats, not him and Rodelle. "Let's see what Connor's up to."

"Itemizing a list of every possible piece of equipment and medicine New Eden could ever need is my guess, and figuring out the best way to convince other medics to move here is another," said Brandon.

James looked at him, like he was surprised Brandon was paying attention. "I guess. Want to see the hospital? It's pretty nice."

"Do you think Connor will be there? It's getting late. He could be in his house."

"He said his house is falling down around his ears and prefers the hospital right now, so I'm looking there. Plus, he said before that my cats will have to be neutered, but I don't know when that should happen, so I want to ask about that."

"That's a good point," Rodelle said. "I want to know too."

"He'll be there," said James confidently.

The kitten in Brandon's arms had fallen asleep by the time they arrived at the hospital, its door wide open. The structure smelled of antiseptic and beneath it, the distinct rubbery fragrance of superboard, the synthetic, weather-proof material that made up the hospital's walls. The all-white foyer split off into three short corridors that led in opposite directions. It was a standard pre-fab hospital unit, so Brandon knew that one corridor led to a small surgical theater and another to a standard examination room for routine appointments. The third corridor would lead to two small private rooms for patient convalescence, and another larger one holding four beds with standard auto-healing units for minor to moderate injuries. It was in this room that they found Connor, fussing over one of the units. The cyborg looked up, his dark brows furrowed in concentration. "Is something wrong with your eyes?" he asked James in greeting.

"Nah, they're good. We came by to ask about neutering."

"For yourself or the cats?"

"Look at you, making a joke," said James. "The cats, obviously."

"We have several weeks before it will become a necessity. The kittens are the equivalent age of ten weeks. This gives me time to learn how to become a veterinarian." Connor glared at the unit. "This is not sufficient for all the needs of New Eden. If this place is to be a home for cyborgs and the Si'laar, we must have appropriate medical procedures in place for both species. The Si'laar are looking forward to expanding their family here, and damned if I can figure out how to make that happen with what we have."

"Korjek and the rest are at the agri-center with Rhys and Hannah, if you want to stop by," Rodelle suggested.

"They are still sorting out their underwater habitat. I'll wait." Exasperated, Connor looked at one of the orange kittens sitting on the floor, licking a leg that was held straight up in the air. For a few seconds, his expression softened. Just as quickly, it was gone. "Do not mind my complaints. I'm otherwise happy with this facility, and it will make a fine hospital once I have all the equipment I need." He made an adjustment to a bed's dome-shaped cover. Suddenly, he froze, his eyes going blank in a way that told Brandon a cyborg was speaking to him. A shadow crossed over his face.

"What's happening?" whispered a horrified James. "Why are his eyes like that?"

"Someone's talking to him." Brandon tripped his brain's cybernetics, uploading himself into the cyborgs' shared link for the first time in what felt like forever.

Darius's voice was grim. *There's been an accident. Get to the ship immediately. And someone has to get Pauline.*

Brandon's stomach turned over. He met Rodelle's anxious gaze. "What happened?" she asked worriedly.

Connor was already sprinting out of the hospital. Brandon fought the urge to follow him, instead handing the kitten back to Rodelle. "I have to go," he said. "Your friend, Pauline? Where would she be?"

"Probably at her house. Why?"

"Look, I don't know yet, but Darius told me there was an accident on our ship and to get Pauline. I'm going to the ship to see what happened. Can you get Pauline?"

Rodelle's eyes were wide with fright, but she nodded. "Yes."

———

JAMES, bless him, held on to her kitten as Rodelle dashed through the settlement to Pauline's house. Since it was on the west side of New Eden, close to the cemetery, it took longer than she wanted, even with running as fast as her legs could carry her. When she arrived, she saw that Jasmine was already there, running in the same direction Rodelle had just come from, Pauline beside her, face was streaked with tears. "Do you know what happened?" Jasmine asked when she saw Rodelle.

Rodelle shook her head. "No, just that I was told to get you and take you to the ship. Connor and Brandon said there was an accident."

"Simon said the same thing before he took off. Darius told everyone." Jasmine sounded out of breath.

"Let's fucking go!" Pauline screamed. "Who cares about who told who?" She started running again, Jasmine and Rodelle at her heels.

Rodelle's legs ached when they reached the ship, but she scarcely noticed it when it came into view, its exterior ramp extended. Darius was waiting for them, his face unnaturally pale, lines bracketing his mouth and eyes. "Pauline." He said her name with a gravitas he'd never had before in Rodelle's memory, with no trace of his usual mirth. Jasmine shrank back a little bit, clearly startled at the change in her boyfriend.

"Where's Aiden?" Pauline asked, voice wobbling.

Was that AL16's new name? Rodelle hadn't known he'd taken one.

"Pauline, I'm so sorry."

"*Where is Aiden?*" She sounded nearly shrill, then bolted up the ramp, trying to get onboard the ship. Darius blocked her way. He blinked, as if fighting back tears.

"There was an electrical short that connected with his internal organs while he was changing out some wires . . ."

"Where is he?" she demanded again, before her face crumpled as a fresh wave of tears flooded her cheeks.

"Oh, my God," said Jasmine. Rodelle felt much the same, knowing what Darius was going to confirm but hoping she was wrong.

Darius's reply was anguished. "Pauline, I wish I didn't have to tell you this, but he . . . they're inside now, preparing to clone him again."

"What?"

"Aiden passed away. He didn't survive the short."

Even though Rodelle knew that Darius was going to deliver terrible news, hearing the words aloud shook her to her core. Her legs nearly gave way. When she looked at Jasmine, she saw her friend looked the same as she felt. Behind her, she was dimly aware of Hannah calling out, but couldn't bring herself to turn around.

"Do what you did for Rhys," Pauline said, voice steely. "You saved him when his brain failed. You can do it for Aiden."

"Rhys was still alive." Darius's voice was hoarse, like he was fighting off tears. "Aiden is . . . he isn't. Pauline, I'm so . . ."

"If you say you're sorry one more time, I will personally take you apart, piece by piece," snarled Pauline. Darius flinched but didn't respond. "Let me see him. Let me see what's left of him, now."

Her voice, though obviously clogged by tears, brooked no argument. Darius nodded. "Yes, of course." He stepped aside, letting Pauline into the ship.

Not sure what to do, Rodelle lingered behind outside, Jasmine next to her. Hannah stepped between them. "Rhys said—well, I'm sure you can guess."

Tears welled in Rodelle's eyes. "There was an accident. Aiden didn't make it."

"Rhys said they're all working to clone him again. I guess they all have to help," Hannah said quietly. "Korjek offered to help, but I don't think the cyborgs wanted it."

Rodelle glanced behind them, noting for the first time the Si'laar contingent standing a few meters away out of respect. Tibbot nodded at them in greeting. Korjek's head was bowed, as if in prayer. "Should we go in?" she asked.

Hannah shook her head. "I don't think that's a good

idea. We don't want to get in the way. I think we should wait here for Pauline. She'll need us."

"Yeah," said Jasmine, sniffling. Hannah reached out and grasped each of their hands.

She wasn't sure how much time passed before Pauline stumbled out of the ship, glassy-eyed and shaking. Spotting the three of them waiting, she dissolved into tears. Through her sobs, she said, "He's gone."

ABOUT THE AUTHOR

Jessica Marting is a sci-fi and paranormal romance author, art enthusiast (not quite an artist, despite all that time in art school), an avid reader, and makeup collector. She lives in Toronto.

Sign up for her newsletter at jessicamarting.com/newsletter for pre-order alerts, sales, freebies, and more.

Standalone Novels & Novellas

Spindle's End

Trade Secrets

Neon Vice

Dead Ringer

Rapture

Escape From Europa 10

Castaways

Demon's Favor

Her Purrfect Match